D0917464

SPECIAL MESSAGE TO READERS

THE ULVERSCROFT FOUNDATION
(registered UK charity number 264873)
was established in 1972 to provide funds for
research, diagnosis and treatment of eye diseases.
Examples of major projects funded by
the Ulverscroft Foundation are:-

- The Children's Eye Unit at Moorfields Eye Hospital, London
- The Ulverscroft Children's Eye Unit at Great Ormond Street Hospital for Sick Children
- Funding research into eye diseases and treatment at the Department of Ophthalmology, University of Leicester
- The Ulverscroft Vision Research Group, Institute of Child Health
- Twin operating theatres at the Western Ophthalmic Hospital, London
- The Chair of Ophthalmology at the Royal Australian College of Ophthalmologists

You can help further the work of the Foundation
by making a donation or leaving a legacy.
Every contribution is gratefully received. If you
would like to help support the Foundation or
require further information, please contact:

**THE ULVERSCROFT FOUNDATION
The Green, Bradgate Road, Anstey
Leicester LE7 7FU, England
Tel: (0116) 236 4325
website: www.foundation.ulverscroft.com**

DREAMS IN THE NIGHT

Tiring of her repressed life on a country farm, teenage beauty Alice Graham runs away from home, hoping to find a job as a journalist in New York in the Roaring Twenties. When her money runs out and she is on the edge of despair, she is befriended by Maddie, a veteran of the burlesque theatre, who takes her under her wing. But Alice soon attracts the unwelcome attentions of a New York gangster, which begins a chain of events that ignites a powder keg of murder and ultimate tragedy . . .

NORMAN FIRTH

DREAMS IN THE NIGHT

Complete and Unabridged

LINFORD
Leicester

First published in Great Britain

First Linford Edition
published 2017

A catalogue record for this book is available
from the British Library.

ISBN 978–1–4448–3526–7

Published by
F. A. Thorpe (Publishing)
Anstey, Leicestershire

Set by Words & Graphics Ltd.
Anstey, Leicestershire
Printed and bound in Great Britain by
T. J. International Ltd., Padstow, Cornwall

This book is printed on acid-free paper

1

The Inside Story

You may have heard of me, and then again you may not. If you have, maybe you'll remember me from the newspaper reports about me killing a guy one night in . . .

But wait a minute; I'm skipping ahead too far, I guess.

At the time of the trial, and later, after I'd been acquitted, there were dozens of news-rags after me, all wanting the inside and exclusive story. But I wouldn't do it — no, not for any of the fabulous prices they offered me for just a page of material written by me personally. I wouldn't do it because right then my life was a hell, what with folks prying on me, pointing me out, and even insulting me to my face. They didn't think I should have been acquitted — they didn't know the true facts, that's why. And I wouldn't write them then because I'd had all the poking and prying I could take and then some.

But it's different now; it all happened twenty years ago, and that's why I'm writing it all down, to let folks see what really went on that night in the luxurious room above the Bexton Burlesque Theatre. And now — to give it you straight, I need the money . . .

I was just a kid then; sixteen, fresh up from the country, where my folks were a couple of respectable, hard-working farm people. On the strength of a high school education, I got ideas about making myself a career; I wanted to bust into journalism, though I had no notion how tough that was. I ran out on them just after my sixteenth birthday, buying a ticket to New York with money I'd been saving for a long time. In those days New York was full of runaway kids, and I didn't have any worries about being traced. I'd changed my name from Alice Graham to Lucille Barry, because I liked the second one better — it had a kind of French sound about it to my ears, and I looked kind of French — I thought — in a blonde way.

Since it happened so long ago, I don't have to act modest in describing myself to you, as I was then. I was big for sixteen — farm life does that for you. I had wide, curving hips and plumply attractive legs, rosy pink; and many a time I'd been taken for a girl of twenty. My hair was natural corn-blonde, the kind the boys like a lot if it's dressed right, and I took care mine always was. On top of that I used to get told by the country hicks down home that I walked in a way that made them fairly drool at the mouth — seductive was the very word. I kind of made them over-ambitious whenever I was alone with any of them.

But I was an innocent kid, just the same. I didn't have any illusions about gooseberry bushes and storks, but at the same time my old mother hadn't told me a thing about what makes the world go around. I knew boys could be bad — but I wasn't quite sure how bad. I knew that the small thrill I used to get when one of the local lads kissed or embraced me wasn't decent. But that's all I did know

— and I came to New York, of all places, like that!

I spent my first couple of nights at the Y.W.C.A., where they didn't seem to ask many questions in those days. I spent my first couple of days looking for a job on a paper or magazine as anything, even an office cleaner.

And I found it wasn't that easy. Nobody in the publishing racket wanted a kid fresh from high school. One old editor did suggest to me that I came along to his apartments and acted as his 'evening secretary;' but since I had a fair idea of what he meant by that, I steered clear.

After three days I had to move out of the Y.W.C.A., since I didn't even have enough to pay the small charge they made. There I was, adrift in New York, wandering along down the East Side by the river, wondering why I was ever silly enough to leave home and take my chances in the outside world. I didn't know what they'd do to me if I was picked up; but I thought, being so young, maybe they'd put me in a reform school. And I was frightened of that, plenty.

I found a cheap hash-house when I'd wandered as far as the Bowery, and I was starving. The sign outside — 'As much as you can get outside of for fifty cents' — made my mouth water, and made me finger my last remaining seventy cents in my pocket. It was a rough kind of dump, but you aren't so fussy when your stomach feels as if it'd make a good stand-in for a big drum. So in I went, my seventy cents clutched tight in my fist, my eyes moving round nervously.

There weren't so many people in there: a few bums drinking coffee from dirty cups, two sailors pouring rum into their cups from flasks they carried, and five or six blowsy women of uncertain ages sitting at stools along the dirty counter, their legs crossed showing a touch of black lacy underthings. I'd heard about women like that, and I couldn't help shuddering with disgust as I passed them and went to the counter. They handed me hard — very hard — looks.

There was plenty of choice. I started with noodle soup, went on to ham with french fries, and then tucked into something they called Bowery pie with beans. None of the food was good, but I guess I was too hungry to give a damn about that. I kept right on eating until I was full up to the back teeth. You see, I wasn't forgetting this might be my last meal for days!

There was peach ice-cream to follow, but even I couldn't eat this, because the milk it had been made from was good and sour. So I took in some crackers and cheese, then sat drinking coffee while one of the sailors, half-drunk, tinkled the keys of an old piano that stood in one corner.

Another guy kept looking over at me, and there was a look in his eyes I didn't like. He looked too almighty fresh to me, and I tried to ignore his gaze. But I couldn't. His eyes fascinated me, so that I had to look over at him — and smile. That was all he needed; he got up and lurched across, leaning by me on the counter. He said: 'Hiya, kid. What're you havin'?'

'Nothing, thanks,' I told him, getting a bit scared at the way the other dames were leering at us. 'I'm full.'

He eyed me speculatively. 'You look like you need something to liven you up. Here, try this . . . ' And he poured rum from his flask into my half-cup of coffee.

I shook my head, but he grinned and pushed it towards me. I did feel I needed a stimulant of some sort, and I'd never tasted intoxicants — so I drunk it, and spent the next five minutes tryin' to get my breath back again.

The sailor laughed at me and said: 'My name's Tom. How they call you, kid?'

'I — I — my name's Alic — I mean Lucille. Lucille Barry.'

My head was spinning by now, and I felt if I didn't get out I was going to be sick right there. So, at his suggestion, I allowed him to steer me from the table towards the door. As we passed the other women, one of them sneered at him and said: 'Cradle robbin', sailor boy? Mind you don't get in trouble, palsy.'

He gave her a wink and chuckled. 'I like 'em young, lady.'

She threw back some nasty crack but we missed it, for the door swung shut behind us on her words. He slid an arm round my waist and started leading me down the dark side streets of the Bowery.

The rum was giving me hell, and we'd only gone a hundred yards when it didn't hold any longer. I had to stop, lean against the wall and vomit. I felt awful and ashamed, but he didn't seem upset about it; he kept his hands on me, holding me with my head bent down while I spluttered and retched. Finally he said: 'Feel better now, baby?'

I felt disgusted with him and myself, and pale and tired. I just wanted somewhere to lie down and sleep to get over the awful feeling my first liquor bout had given me. I mumbled: 'Please go away now, please. Thank you for helping me, but I'm all right now. Just leave me here.'

His eyes narrowed and he looked incredulous. He said: 'Hey, what the hell you givin' me, you cheap floozie? Whaddya mean, beat it? Like hell I will.'

I was soberer now. I'd lost the drink; I stared at him in sheer horror. It was all clear to me just what I'd gotten myself into, and I trembled all through my body.

I was innocent all right, but a girl from the city had once told me just what sailors are, and this one was living up to that reputation. He gripped my arm so hard it made me wince with agony.

I tried to struggle free and cried: 'Let me go or I'll scream for help.'

'That's a laugh. Who'd help you? The cops are too scared to come down here in case they get a lead filling. A dame can scream her head off hereabouts and nobody thinks a thing of it. Go ahead, see if I ain't right.'

And he pulled me to him forcibly and thrust his unshaven face towards mine, pressing his thick, blubbery lips hard and brutally on my face. I screamed and kicked — kicked so it hurt, and watched him stagger back, groaning. I was frightened of what I'd done then; fear held me rooted there, trembling and shaking at the idea of what he'd do to me when he recovered, but totally unable to move a muscle.

His eyes were almost murderous when he came at me again; his hands were making claws, claws that were reaching out for me, for God knows what purpose. He grated: 'You little bitch — I'll strangle you!'

I managed to scream loudly then, and he sneered. 'You asked for trouble, babe, and I'm the guy to give it to you. And if you try anything else like kicking, I'll . . . '

Then I saw the woman loom out of the shadows behind him and hit him viciously with a bottle she held. The bottle smashed on his head, and a reek of cheap whisky hit the atmosphere. But the sailor went down without a murmur, full out on the floor, a trickle of blood seeping down his temple from his thick black hair. The woman glared down at him, raised her foot, and kicked him brutally in the chest. Then she looked at me and her glance softened up.

'Poor kid,' she said. 'How'd you get tangled up with a bum like this?'

'I — I don't know. He — gave me liquor . . . '

'Sure, they always do. Well, you push off home now, honey, 'fore he comes round. And stay away from the Bowery at night if you aim to duck this kinda trouble. Understand? Go on, get home, quick.'

Her mention of home finished me; I just burst into one long kiddish wail right there in the street.

'What the hell?' she said, amazed. 'Nothin' to cry over now, is there? Or maybe you're afraid your old man'll give it to you when he spots your torn dress?'

'No, no, it isn't that,' I cried. 'It's just that I — I haven't any — any home to go to. I'm all alone here.'

Her face softened still more; she said: 'How'd that happen?'

'I — I ran away from the small town I lived in, thinking I'd make a career for myself down here — only — only it wasn't so easy.'

'It never is, kid. What was your line? You want to crash the stage, or be a photographer's model? A mannequin?'

'No. I wanted to be — to be a — reporter.'

She smiled at that, took a handkerchief out of her pocket and wiped my eyes. The sailor down there started to groan and stir, and she said: 'You better come with

11

me for now. That bum'll be raving mad when he snaps out of it. Come on, then. Come along to my place an' you c'n tell Maddie all about it, huh? Oh, sure, I almost forgot — my name's Maddie Maritza — I get bill space down at Foley's Burlesque Theatre. What's yours?'

'My real name's Alice Graham, but I call myself Lucille Barry.'

As we walked away with her arm round my shoulders, she said: 'Say, that's a regular professional name — maybe Tim could find you a job at the theatre. We'll have to see!'

2

Four a Day!

Maddie Maritza's rooms were just off the Bowery. They weren't luxurious, but they were comfortable and homely. The walls were practically papered with photographs of men, most of them signed with things like 'To Gorgeous, with love and memories' and 'What a night — I'll be back, lovely,' and so on.

She made coffee, and while we drank it I said: 'You certainly know a lot of men, Maddie.'

'Men? Oh, those guys. Just playboys and sugar daddies. None of them mean a thing to me. I haven't yet met a guy who I'd like to settle down with — maybe I never will at that. Those mugs are good for what I can get out of them; but once they find they're not going to get a thing out of me, they blow double fast.'

'You mean — you fool them?'

'Sure, string them along. It's a philosophy, kid. To dames like me that's what men are there for — suckers they are, all of 'em. They're okay for having yourself a time, but once their wallets are empty and their billfolds get that flabby look, it's high time to back out.'

'Don't you ever have trouble with any of them?'

'Sure; but I can handle seven different kinds of trouble. You saw how I handled your sailor friend, didn't you?'

I regarded her admiringly. I guess right then I felt what almost added up to heroine worship for her. She was getting along, must have been about thirty-two or three, but careful use of make-up brought her age down to round about twenty-eight or so. There was lots of hardness to her face, but there was kindliness and humour in her eyes, and a merry curve to her scarlet lips. She wore her hair up, on her head, and suited that style immensely. Her legs, which were folded under her, were shapely and long, without an ounce of superfluous fat on them, but very far from being skinny. Her waist was very slim, slimmer even than mine, and the dress she wore accented the slenderness.

That was Maddie Maritza, strip artiste from Foley's Burlesque stand — not rating any great honours in her own game, but a useful and ever-popular turn with the tired businessmen and the young, silly adolescent kids who haunted the burlesque joints. That was Maddie, from whom I learned the elementary technique of making the most of my appeal to men, and how to safeguard myself when I'd used that appeal to full advantage. Yes, I almost worshipped her — even wanted to be like her at that time. I thought her life was exciting and attractive. Since then I've found out it's exciting enough, but about the attractiveness I can't be sure.

Anyway, read on; maybe you can form your own opinions about that in time.

She said: 'Before we get talking, suppose we make ourselves comfortable in some other clothes?'

'I — I haven't anything suitable for — comfort. No dressing robe or anything of that kind.'

15

'That's okay. I'll loan you one of mine. The one that big oil well owner bought me oughta suit you okay. It's too young for me. I'm getting scraggy around the neck — haveta wear a high-necked creation these days to keep kidding myself I'm still young.'

She swept into the bedroom and came back dressed in a powder-blue negligee that showed her graceful figure to full advantage. She brought me a green creation in soft, clinging silk, and a fluffy robe that enhanced rather than hid it. I undressed while she talked and slipped the nightgown on, putting the negligee over it.

She was looking at me admiringly all the time, and at last when I sat down, she said: 'Baby, what I wouldn't give for your youth, looks and figure! *Wow!*'

I blushed a little; I wasn't used to such frank comments from members of my own sex. Mother had always taught me the body was something to be ashamed of, and I guess that view stuck to me more or less. I had really been embar-rassed about taking my things off in front

16

of her, but hadn't liked to say so.

'How old are you, kid?' she asked suddenly. 'I'd say you were maybe eighteen, nineteen.'

'No. I've really only just turned sixteen,' I told her.

'Hmm. Why'd you run away?'

'Well, it was so — so slow at home. I hated the local boys — all except one — and I wanted to make good for myself on my own.'

'The old, old story,' she sighed. 'That's how it happened with me. Only I was lucky, see. Lots of clever dames like me wind up trampin' the streets and selling themselves for a living. They find it's the only way they can live without working hard. I don't want you to finish that way.'

'I — I know. I'd sooner kill myself than that. I — I saw some of the kind you mean, tonight. Horrible.'

She looked at me up and down quizzically. 'Suppose I paid your fare back home? Would you go?'

I hesitated. Then I shook my head slowly. 'I wouldn't like to — I do so want to stay here in the city. But, I suppose, I'll have to . . . '

Maybe she could hear the weariness in my voice; see it in my eyes. She could tell I didn't want to go back again. I wasn't sure how my parents would react, for one thing — they were very strict. On top of that, I remembered her remark about Tim finding me a job at the theatre. I thought she'd forgotten about that, but now she said: 'What do you think of burlesque?'

'I hadn't thought about it at all,' I stammered.

'Hmm. I'm wondering how a kid like you'd react to that kind of thing. I expect it'd seem pretty raw to you, wouldn't it?'

'In what way?'

'Well, for one thing, you're self-conscious about your body. You wouldn't like displaying it to a bunch of tired businessmen.'

I had to think this over. I looked at her. 'I don't know. Just how far would I have to go?'

'That depends on the show you get into. There's a dump down in Hell's Kitchen where you only wear a pleasant smile. But Tim Foley never lets his girls go so far. Generally we keep our courage up with the aid of a G-string and a brassiere strap . . . although our star does go the whole hog, with a quick blackout to shield her. Now what do you think? Could you go for *that* — or would you rather beat it back to Mom and Pop?'

I shivered. 'I'm not sure — but I think I could do that, rather than — than have to go back home with my tail between my legs, like a young fool.'

'I see what you mean. Well, if you can take it, the pay isn't bad. You have to get used to regarding the audience as so many fat fools, so many lumps of wood, who're paying good money to see a body beautiful. You mustn't start putting personal angles into your work.'

I nodded.

'You'd naturally be embarrassed at first, but that passes. How do you think you'd stand up to four-a-days?'

'Four-a-days? What's that?'

'Sure, you wouldn't know, would you. Four-a-days are four nonstop perfor-mances each day. You damn near live in the theatre, but that isn't so bad. You get lots of laughs, and the girls are a nice bunch once you get to know them. And Sunday's free. It isn't like being on tour, where you're travelling all day Sunday and working every weekday. But it is grueling at times. Think you could stand up to that?'

'I think so. I had to work pretty hard on our farm at harvest time. Yes, it wouldn't affect me.'

'Then you should be okay. You'll be a bit soft at first, but as long as you watch yourself with the stage-door wolves you'll be all right. In time you'll develop the regulation cash register heart, and only go out with a guy for what you can get out of him, and not vice versa. But for the first six months you'll need to watch yourself. In fact, you'd better stick close to me at nights when we leave. How'd you like to live here with me?'

'I'd love that.'

'Then it's settled. We'll work it that way. And always remember, I'll only hand you good advice — and take it. Don't get high and mighty too soon.'

'Oh I won't, I promise. But — but aren't you going a bit too far ahead? How do you know Tim Foley will take me?'

'Honey,' said Maddie, cynically, glancing up and down my form, 'I'd like to see Tim Foley turn down anyone with a figure like yours!'

⋆   ⋆   ⋆

She was right. I found that out about Maddie very quickly. Where men and their reactions were concerned, she was *always* right. Perhaps if I'd taken her advice like she said, a bit later on, I'd never have had to stand trial for murder. But you think of these things too late . . .

Tim Foley was a large, fat, Western-looking character. He wore a Stetson hat, and a wide smile that showed his gold-filled front teeth. He had a habit of always hooking his thumbs into his belt, and a hoarse, sometimes squeaky, voice, like a man perpetually suffering from a bad cold.

His theatre was a small affair, with lurid bills outside of it, showing beautiful girls about to come clean. The bill matter read: 'Girls, *Girls*, GIRLS! Twenty of them, and every one a true American beauty.' Maddie was featured in one full-size portrait, wearing nothing at all but a coy smile, and with her back to the camera, her features peeking coyly over one smooth shoulder. She pointed to it and said: 'Taken about ten years ago — that's helped to draw a hell of a lot of custom at that.'

We went in the stage entrance around the back and came onto the stage. A harassed-looking middle-aged man was directing about a dozen chorines in a dance routine. He was shouting: 'Come on, girls, pep it up. Hell, you ain't training for a funeral march. Get your legs up — you're supposed to be high-kicking, not stepping over a body in the roadway. Snap it up!'

The piano tinkled out, and the line of perspiring girls went into the routine again. I whispered to Maddie: 'Gosh, I couldn't do *that*.'

She patted my hand. 'Relax, kid. You don't have to. That's only the regular specialty troupe. The chorus is different again; they're showgirls that you're going into. They don't have to be clever — long as they look good, are tall, and move gracefully.'

She took me down the steps at the centre of the stage, ignoring the dancers. Sitting in the third row back, wearing an expansive beam, was Tim Foley. His fancy waistcoat bulged over his huge stomach, and he was chewing an unlighted cigar. But his face was plump and kindly, and good-humoured. As Maddie approached, he stood up courteously, bowed to her then said: 'Where in hell have you been, Maddie? We've been holding up the 'Devil Dance' number waitin' for you.'

'Relax, Tim; take it easy. I've found a little something for you. Meet Miss Lucille Barry.'

'Yeah?' His eyes shifted to me, and a look of pleasure dawned in them. 'It's a pleasure, Miss Barry.'

'She'd like a job,' Maddie told him. 'So she's giving you first chance. Better jump to it, Tim, or someone else'll snap her up.'

23

'Yeah, sure, sure.' He looked at me keenly. 'Ever been in burlesque before?'

'No,' I replied nervously. 'I'm sorry . . .'

'Skip it; it doesn't really matter a lot. How old are you?'

'She's twenty,' put in Maddie quickly.

Tim said: 'You let her do her own answering, Maddie.'

'That's right — I'm twenty,' I lied quickly.

'Hmm. Mind showing me your legs, Miss Barry?'

I blushed and looked at Maddie. She nodded encouragingly, and I raised my skirts above my knees a little.

Tim said: 'I meant your legs, not your ankles, Miss Barry. Higher please.'

Even that was an ordeal for me, and I edged my skirt up very slowly, until, when it was about a foot above the knee, he said:

'Okay, swell. That's enough. So you'd like to join the showgirls, would you?'

Maddie put in: 'I been thinking, Timmy. How about trying her for a strip spot? You only got three strippers besides the stars, and dern near every other theatre stocks at least six. What say?'

'Without any experience? You're nuts.'

'Why not try her? She's got looks and shape. It's only a question of graceful movement, and she's no hayseed when it comes to that.'

He nodded thoughtfully. 'Yeah, she'd be a draw. But can she carry it off?'

'She can try — can't you, honey?'

I said I could.

'Okay,' agreed Tim. 'Take her backstage and fix her up with one of your costumes. Then bring her back along for an audition.'

While I changed in the dressing room, I felt my courage gradually ebbing. Maddie said: 'If you get this spot, it means a break for you and a wage packet three times as big. Just take off as gracefully and rhythmically as you can to the music. If you click, Tim'll have someone train you properly. Good luck, honey.'

I got on the stage, moving in time with the tinkling piano. I slid off my shoulder straps, started shivering the dress down — then I spotted Tim and the dance director, and the pianist, all gaping at me, and I knew I couldn't go through with it. Burning with shame, I pushed the straps back and rushed off the stage!

3

Cigars — Cigarettes!

I was trembling as I dressed in the deserted dressing rooms. I hadn't missed seeing the grins on the faces of some of the girls and stagehands when I had rushed off, and I felt terribly ashamed of myself for it. It hadn't even been as though there'd been an audience — but it was no use. I just couldn't detach myself from the fact that people were looking at me disrobing. It was my training coming out on top!

What would Maddie say about it, after pleading with Timmy to give me a spot? She'd be disgusted with me — my ears burned at the thought of what she must even then be saying to Foley in front. I decided to get dressed and slink away without seeing her again, and facing her recriminations. I felt I had let her down badly.

She walked in just as I was drawing on my stockings, and stood leaning against the door watching me. She didn't speak, and I couldn't tell from her face what she was thinking. I stammered: 'I — I'm awfully sorry, Maddie — after all you did for me . . . '

'What went wrong?' she asked.

'I don't know — just the idea of it — Tim Foley and the dance director, and the stagehands . . . I couldn't do it.'

'Foley? Good God, kid, he looks on girls as he'd look on a new car. For the performance he'd get out of them.'

'I know — I know.' I nodded miserably. 'It's just me — I'm a silly fool. But perhaps it's as well it happened now rather than with a regular audience. I suppose you're very mad at me?'

She grinned and walked across to pat my shoulder. 'Hell, no! If you're a decent enough kid not to want to show your figure to a bunch of old screwballs, who am I to be mad at you? I kinda admire you in one way — except that you won't ever get into big money being so scrupulous about yourself. But forget that

— big money isn't everything, not by one hell of a long way it ain't. You'll marry some nice punk kid and settle down and raise a family — maybe. An' you'll be a damn sight happier than you would be in this lousy game.'

I was grateful for her words, but it didn't help right then. As she said I might marry and settle down and give a career a miss at some time in the future, but the future seemed an awful long way off right then. Meanwhile, I thought my flopping this job meant home for me, and I felt pretty badly about the whole thing. I'd even have tried the strip act again if they'd have let me — but I guess the same thing would have happened at that.

There was a sudden rap on the door, and Tim Foley walked in. 'Hello, kid. All dressed.'

'Yes, Mr. Foley. I — I'm sorry about causing you all this trouble for nothing,' I told him, blushing.

'Think nothing of it, Miss Barry. You ain't the first who's gotten cold feet at the last minute. It ain't your fault.'

Maddie said: 'Listen, Tim, how about

giving the kid a chance with the showgirls? Maybe it's just the idea of stripping she can't take?'

He shook his head decidedly. 'Guess not, Maddie. Some of the numbers the chorus cuties do are warmish — how about the 'Living Statues' ensemble? Nope, I'm afraid we've got nothing in the show for her — but I have got a suggestion, if she's wanting a job.'

'I am, Mr. Foley,' I told him eagerly. 'Anything.'

'It ain't much, and the dough's poor, but it'd help you along for the time being, until you grab off this reportin' old Maddie's been telling me you want.'

'I'll take it,' I said eagerly. 'I don't mind what it is.'

'You don't mind sellin' cigars and cigarettes?'

It was a bit of a damper, but I was grateful. I felt badly about having come to New York cocksure and full of plans for a career as a distinguished journalist, and then to have to trot round a burlesque theatre selling smokes. But it was the only way out, and the only job to be had right then. Add to that the fact that I'd already grown to like the atmosphere of the theatre, and you won't need two guesses to know I clinched the offer on the spot.

'It carries ten bucks a week, that's all,' explained Tim. 'Can you manage on that?'

'Sure she can — she's rooming with me,' explained Maddie. 'We'll split the rent — it'll only cost her one buck a week for her share.'

I was surprised that her rooms came so cheap. Later I found out the actual rent was six dollars a week — but that was Maddie all over; she had a heart as big as it could possibly be, and very often she didn't even take the dollar if she could possibly kid me into keeping it without embarrassing me. And so it was fixed up — I was working at Foley's Burlesque Theatre; not, then, as a prime attraction, but as a lowly cigarette girl. I often wonder if I'd known what a change that was going to make to my life, whether I'd have taken the job, or run home like a startled rabbit!

There's something about a burlesque

theatre that gets you when the lights are up, and the red-nosed comic has the audience rolling in the aisles, and everyone's happy and carefree. The highbrows can say what they like, and the longhairs can elevate their well-blown noses at burlesque, but that's just an act on their part. If they unbuttoned and attended a burlesque performance just once, I'll guarantee they'd make a weekly trip of it in the future.

My first week at Foley's was the most exciting week I'd had in my entire life — up to then, of course. It was fascinating to watch the types who came — we got everything from Park Avenue debs, and playboys, to Bowery thugs and their 'dolls'. Some of them were even ordinary, good-class people; young college men out on a bender, factory hands, shop assistants. Those were the funniest. They were mostly ashamed to be spotted going into a girl show; you could see them walk slowly past the front of the house, then turn around and saunter back. They'd stand by the photo frames as if they were waiting for someone, and take a casual look at the photographs pinned outside. You could almost see their eyes gleaming and their mouths watering. Then, when they thought no one was looking, they'd suddenly gallop furtively in, slam down their money, get their seat, and slink down in it until the lights went low. But once the show started, they got just as boisterous as the rest of the audience.

The cigarette-selling job was swell; I liked it. Often I got good tips, and always I met interesting people. At first I was nearly too ashamed to walk down the aisle, for the uniform that went with the job was one of the briefest things I ever saw. I was darned glad it wasn't winter. The skirt of black silk only fell a matter of six inches from the waist, and the bosom of the top was cut so low you could almost count every rib I had. But I gathered my courage, and eventually I realised there was so much going on — or should I say coming off? — on the stage, that folks hardly even noticed me. I got used to it.

Things went on that way for what

seemed a long time to me. Maybe you've noticed yourself how slow the years pass until you hit twenty or twenty-one, then you'd like to hold them back if you could, but you can't. After that age time slips away so you hardly even notice it going.

A lot of things happened to make me a queen of burlesque; and I guess one of the most important was Babe Della's being murdered.

I was right next to the guy when it happened. It all came out later that Babe, the star of the show, had been running him around and giving him hell generally. He was only young, and a good-looking boy, with nice wavy hair and even white teeth. Babe had been playing around with him until she'd gotten him in that state where he didn't know whether he was going or coming. Then she'd given him the brush-off for a fat slug from the city with a wallet stacked out with greenbacks.

The kid was cut up, and he'd argued with her some, but hadn't made any headway. Babe was one of those green-eyed, red-haired mommas, hot as they come, drifting around from one sucker to the next. The boy had been fun while he'd lasted, but she was through now, and he should have known better than to haunt her. He was sure to get hurt.

But this night he was in front, and he'd sent red orchids to her dressing room, with a note pleading with her. Babe was a funny girl, and had some funny ways. She was fed up with his attentions, and she meant to show him once and for all she was through. She picked a lousy way of doing it, and it's no wonder the kid went mad — although I figured myself he'd meant to kill her anyway, otherwise why the revolver he carried with him so conveniently?

Anyhow, the way she picked to show him what she now thought of him was simply to lean forward after her act and throw the orchids right in his face from the rundown platform that led out into the centre aisle. The yahoos in front laughed like hell, and then she turned her back, unsnapped one of her garters, and threw it to the new boyfriend who was seated opposite. That was right when the boy got very pale — I was hardly three feet from him at the time — drew his gun, and before anyone could stop him, shot Babe twice through the back! Then he turned the gun on himself and pumped a slug into his brainbox, to settle the matter for always.

Babe died in considerable pain in her dressing room, about five minutes before we got a doctor. She didn't have anything to say — she wasn't able to speak. But the current boyfriend didn't show his greasy mug within a mile of her, obviously being afraid of any undesirable publicity being given to him.

But Babe's death meant that Maddie got top billing in the show. Which, in turn, meant one of the chorines got Maddie's solo spot. Which meant Tim needed a new girl for the chorus. Which was where I stepped in, at Maddie's persuasion.

I stepped in, and carried the audition. I knew the show by heart, even to all the changes of programme. I'd gotten so used to trotting around in my skimpy uniform that the chorus girls had actually looked well dressed in comparison — they did have more on, but it was filmier. However, I was hardening up nicely then.

I ran through several numbers for Tim, and I didn't give a cuss. I worked the can-can, which was a stock part of the show, walking out along the runway into the audience and showing the boys plenty of what they liked and admired. And naturally, the more I appeared, the more used I got to it.

I remembered the boys back home and what they'd said about the way I walked, and I put it on. It wasn't long before I was elevated to doing short gags and sketches with the comedian. Then I got a solo number, singing — I had a low, husky kind of voice, which never failed to get the audience.

That was when I met Corday.

Corday was a big shot around those parts. He owned thousands of pin-tables, and also had a big stake in illicit booze. He was dark and looked like my idea of a movie star, and he had wavy black hair and nice grey eyes. That, added to the fact that his front name was Ricardo — Riccy for short — and the fact that his manners were as elegant as his speech and dress, made him attractive to most girls. I was young and romantic, and I was getting just a little bit fed up with being looked after by Maddie. Maddie always saw me home, then went out herself with her own boyfriends. So it was pretty miserable for me after the show, and I felt entitled to a bit of pleasure.

I remember it was a hot July evening when Corday first spoke to me; I was still plodding upward at the theatre, and had been working there almost a year then. I was doing a number with three other girls, a crazy little tune with the title 'A boy like you could do things to a girl like me!' The audience used to love it, especially when the four of us went down into the front row seats, sat on the guys' knees and kissed them, and let them put their arms around our waists. And I happened to sit on Corday's lap.

He was along with another woman at the time, and she looked at me as if she'd like to have killed me there and then. It didn't worry me, of course, for it was all a part of my act and I never suspected it'd fruit into reality. But Corday rested his hand on my knee while I sang the chorus of the song to him, then said in a low voice: 'What kind of things could a boy like me do to a dish like you, cutie?'

'I could think of things,' I cracked back in the usual way we all do when the fellows we'd chosen tried to get clever. 'And keep your hand right where it is on my knee, will you? Don't get too fresh, stranger.'

He laughed at that. 'I'm sorry, baby. Couldn't resist it at all. You're cute, aren't you? How do they call you?'

'The name's Barry,' I told him.

'What sort of Barry?'

'Lucille.'

'Well listen Lucille, how about . . . ' I didn't hear the rest of what he was going to say, because right then I had to rush to join the rest of the girls back on the stage. But from there on until the show ended, I knew his eyes were on me — and so were the eyes of the woman with him, and did she look mad jealous!

I was telling Maddie about him after the show, and she asked me if I knew who he was. I said no I didn't. She shrugged and told me I should be careful. She had a date herself that night, and she told me to go right home from the theatre before she left me. I might have done that, too, only I was feeling sick of being still a kid. I wanted to have fun — good, clean fun; and when I found Corday waiting outside, that settled it!

4

Not That Kind of Fun!

Corday was standing in the shadows just outside the stage entrance. I came out with two of the other girls who went my way, laughing and chatting. I didn't know he was there until a voice spoke from the shadows, and an arm reached out and hooked into mine. I was jerked to a stop, and since I was linking my two friends, they were halted too.

'Hello, girly,' said Corday with a smile as he stepped into the dim lamplight. 'Thought you'd never get out. Where we going?'

'*Mmm*' exclaimed one of the other two. 'We'll go anyplace you say, handsome.'

'I was speaking to the *lady*,' said Corday, giving her a cold stare. 'Understand?'

'Well, the nerve! What d'you think we are, Bluebeard? Old hags?'

'Exactly,' agreed Corday ever so politely. 'Good night, girls!'

'Well I like that — or rather I don't!' snapped the one who had spoken to him. 'Are you going with that punk, Lucille? Tell him where he gets off.'

I looked at Corday, and he handed me a smile that did things to me. I stammered: 'He — he's an old friend of mine. I think I'll have supper with him.'

'Are you kiddin'? That guy's Ricardo Corday, the bootlegger. He's nobody's friend, not even his own.'

'Just the same, I think I'll go along . . . I'm feeling a bit fed up.'

'You'll be fed up all right when that punk's done with you,' she grunted, glaring at Corday. 'And how.'

Corday said softly and pleasantly: 'Why don't you shut that big rat trap of yours before someone shuts it for you? And why don't you blow while the blowing's good?'

They sniffed, gave him a haughty stare, and blew as he suggested. He allowed a grin to spread over his face as he looked after them, then turned to me and said: 'Take no notice of them, Lucille. Jealous.'

I nodded. They *were* jealous, I could see that. They would have given anything to have been in my shoes. The idea that me, a mere kid, should have important people like Corday pounding the pavement waiting for me, had rattled them some.

'Where'd you like to go?' He smile.

'I don't much mind — Mr. Corday. Anywhere we can have fun.'

'Then we'll start at the Glass Slipper on Forty-second — and call me Riccy, kid. Let's go.'

He had his car waiting around at the end of the alley, and we climbed in and drove off. On the way I said: 'What became of your, er, lady friend?'

'Oh, Mitzi, you mean? Just a has-been.'

'Mitzi?'

'Yeah, Mitzi Larue. Owns the Spotlight Club in the Harlem District. I sometimes get around with her when I haven't got anything more important on my mind. You get me?'

'She seemed mighty jealous,' I told him. 'She looked at me tonight as if she'd like to have killed me.'

'She probably would — wouldn't any woman want to kill some other girl who'd taken me off them?'

I thought he was joking, but a look at his face told me he was quite serious. He really did count himself a killer with the ladies, and took it as natural that the ladies should recognise how good he was being to them by bothering with them at all. But I wasn't one of his usual pick-ups. I detested big-headedness and conceit. I said nastily: 'It's easy to see you think you're God's gift to women.'

He looked at me in surprise. 'Aren't I? Suppose I told you that if you were going to be smart about things, you'd better get out here and start walking yourself home. What would you say to that?'

'I'd say I'd had a lucky escape,' I sneered, thinking he wouldn't really try it. But he did. He braked the car, swung open the door, and barked: 'All right, girlie. Out you get. Been nice knowing you and all the rest of it.'

I just sat and stared at him. He said: 'Now what? Or don't you want to have that lucky escape after all?'

'No,' I whispered. 'Now you mention it, I don't. Maybe you are God's gift to women after all. Drive on.'

'Atta girl.' He grinned, and he did drive on.

We took in the Glass Slipper first of all; but it was dull there, no floor show or anything, just illicit booze served in coffee cups. Riccy soon got tired of it, and suggested we ought to push along. We got in the car again and drove off. This time he left the theatre district altogether and drove down towards Harlem. I hadn't been to Harlem before, but I wasn't very impressed.

He drew up before a place that looked like a tenement house and said: 'Out you get, girlie. Here we are.'

'But — where's this?' I asked, gazing at it blankly.

'I know it looks gruesome from here,' he laughed. 'But down in the basement it's pretty lively. This is the Spotlight Club.'

'The — the one that that — that girl — that Mitzi Larue owns? Oh, but Riccy, aren't you worried about going here? She might start trouble.'

He laughed at that one and hustled me along the path, down some steps to a basement door. He rapped in code on this and it opened for him. A big fellow let us in, smiling. 'How are you tonight, Mister Corday?'

'I'm fine, Washington. Place crowded tonight?'

'We all can't grumble, sir. Folks is a-trickling in all the time. But always room for you! Go right on in.'

He took my arm and led me through a curtain into a room from which the strains of hot jazz were issuing. It was a long, low basement room comprised of several cellars knocked into one another. The walls were painted with startling scenes from past stage shows — probably that was where it derived its name of the Spotlight Club. Its clientele was a mixture of types; black folk predominated, but there were people of all races. Four singing waiters were rendering — or maybe I should say rending! — an old-time quartet, in white beer aprons and shirt sleeves and false whiskers. They

46

cracked on the last note, bowed, and beat it. We found a table for two in a corner and sat down.

'See who's getting up into the band,' said Corday, and I gasped as I spotted one of the most famous black band leaders and trumpet players of the day joining the band.

'Does he work here?' I said in amazement, for I happened to know he was under exclusive contract to a luxury hotel.

'No, he doesn't work here — at least, he doesn't get paid for his playing, if that's what you mean. But lots of the name bands come down here after midnight for a workout, a jam session. Half the gents on the stand there are members of name bands. Wait until they start to give out.'

They started giving out right then; and couples got to their feet and began to dance ecstatically to the rhythm. But that was real playing; and while I drank some hooch Riccy had ordered, I found my feet tapping time to the music, so that at last I said: 'Riccy — Riccy, shall we dance?'

He wasn't too keen, but he got up gracefully and swung me into the congested mass. He danced adequately, and we got around well with each other, neither of us being spectacular. Once in the centre of the heaving mob, we could barely move two inches to either side, so we just stood locked in each other's arms, with Riccy smiling down at me, and me with my head going around a bit from the drink and the heat.

Suddenly I felt his hand pressing me in the small of the back. His lips swooped down and pressed hard upon mine for a moment. Then he rose again and said: 'Nice?'

The burst of applause drowned my reply, which wasn't very flattering. Riccy said: 'Here, come along with me.' He led me to the band platform and climbed up, pushing me before him. He nodded to the members and said to the leader: 'I'd like to sit in at the piano, Al. And the little lady'd like to sing for me, wouldn't you, sweets?'

I stammered a refusal, but he laughed me down. The leader smiled and said:

'Sure thing, Riccy. What'll she sing?'

'How about 'A boy like you could do things to a girl like me!',' suggested Riccy. 'Know it?'

'Sure, we got that one okay.'

'Then strike up.'

Before I knew where I was, I was standing up there giving out with the number, and giving it all I'd got. The crowd stopped dancing to whistle and yell approval. Riccy was doing a bit of clever work on the keys, and when I'd taken the first chorus, he did some improvising that sounded far better to me than many a professional pianist I'd heard. The place rang with applause when we were through, and we slid down again and went back to our seats.

And who should be sitting there but — Mitzi Larue! To me she looked as if she was going to burst wide apart at any given moment. She sat with her hands clenched, her face red, and her heavy bosom heaving with emotion.

Riccy said: 'Hiya, Mitzi. Nice to to see you again. Drinking with me and the little lady?'

'You great big bum,' she breathed murderously. 'How the hell can you dare to try this act with me? What's your idea? D'you think for a minute you can stand me up like this, like you have done, and actually insult me in my own club?'

'I don't get it — don't get it at all,' said Riccy. 'I can't see where *I've* insulted you — *yet*.'

'No? You know damn well everyone here knows I'm nuts about you, and that we were pairing off as a twosome. Now you drop me cold outside the theatre saying you've got business to see to, then you bring this cheap floozie here, in my own club, and show her off to all the customers and the folks who work for me. Do you think that's clever, Riccy, you sleek rat?'

He flushed. 'Listen, I don't like your tone. Maybe I'm getting sick and tired of you. You knew it wouldn't last, didn't you? Now give your big mouth a rest, Mitzi, and blow.'

'You don't get rid of me that easy,' she snapped, going crimson. 'I'm not like the others you've had. I'm no plaything for a guy like you.'

'Don't get steamed up,' said Riccy levelly. 'You've been a plaything for years for one guy or another. Just because you happen to reckon it's time you had a husband, doesn't say I'm going to be the unlucky sap you put a halter around.'

She flared up, forgetting to keep her voice down, and screeched: 'So you're dropping me for a cheap bitch like her? A blasted show-all for tired businessmen, are you? A filthy little . . . *oh*!'

Riccy's open hand had landed full across her face, knocking her back into her chair. She sat and stared at him for a minute. His face was purple with rage, his teeth clenched together. He said: 'I brought this lady along to let you see me and you was through for quits. I'm not standing here to have her insulted. That's all I have to say — and keep out of my way in future, Mitzi.'

He grabbed my arm and started dragging me towards the exit. Mitzi got to her feet and called after me: 'You wait you long-legged bitch! I'll fix you for this, if I

51

take a hundred years about it. Maybe I can't get back at Riccy, but I *can* at *you*. You . . . '

I was glad to get outside in the cool night air; Riccy was trembling and his face was still dark with anger and temper. He said nothing until we were in the car, then he murmured: 'Sorry I took you there, kid. I might've known she'd take it that way.'

'It — it's all right,' I told him. 'She didn't worry me at all.'

'That's the way to take it. I'll take damn good care she doesn't get back at you in any way. Trust me.'

It was dark in the car, but his eyes were wandering over me, and I felt self-conscious under his gaze. I pulled my dress down further over my knees, then he pulled me to him again, said: 'You kiss swell, cutie. Let's have another helping, shall we?'

I submitted to his embrace, although I was feeling rather sick after the scene that had just taken place. I suddenly pushed him away and said: 'Stop it, Riccy. Please.'

'What's hit you? I thought you wanted fun, babe?'

'I do — but I'm tired now. Will you take me home — please, Riccy?'

Without a word, he started the car and drove me homewards.

5

Maddie Gets Het Up

Looking back on the whole thing from where I am now, I can see Maddie was right about Corday that night. She was mad about it when I told her — and at the time I thought she was just jealous like the other girls. I was a damned little fool. I know that now.

Corday left me at the door to our apartments; but before he let me out of the car he pulled me hard against him and pressed kisses on my lips. 'Sorry about what happened tonight, baby,' he said. 'I must've had too much hooch. I'm seeing you again, or am I?'

'I don't know, Riccy. Maybe. Suppose you think it over. I'm not the kind of girl you want, am I? Not really.'

'You mean because of what happened back there? Oh, forget that. Sure you're the kind I want — exactly: I'm getting

54

tired of cheap floozies anyhow. How about me picking you up after the show tomorrow night and taking you some place for supper?'

I thought it over for a minute. He sounded genuinely sorry. 'All right. If you want to.'

'Swell, kid. Sleep tight.'

He was gone then, leaving me staring after the car, swaying a bit from being liquored up, but feeling pretty pleased with myself on the whole. I was thinking that if a guy like Riccy could be interested in a kid like me, hardly out of pigtails, I certainly must have *something*.

At last I fitted my key and walked up the stairs to the top flats. The door was unlocked and I went in, lurching a bit as I did so. I flopped onto the sofa, then I spotted Maddie looking at me funnily — she was sitting in a corner of the window seat, dressed in her negligee and little else on account of the warmth of the night. She still looked lovely to my eyes, but now I was beginning to see where I was every bit as good as her.

'Hi, Maddie,' I said.

Still she didn't answer. She got up and came over, took my shoulders, and shook them hard.

I said: 'Hey, give over that, will you?' and I sniggered in a nasty kind of way.

'Getting quite sassy, aren't you?' she snapped. 'Where've you been?'

'Been? It isn't your business, is it? If you must know, I've been havin' fun. Lotsa fun.'

'You're half-soused.'

'Mmmm. S'nice feelin'. Like it.'

'I said, where've you been, kid?'

'S'none of your business. You keep away from me. Got a right to do what I want, don't I? Been havin' fun.'

I was feeling muzzier every minute; the heat of the room was making my head spin, and every now and again I couldn't resist an impulse to burst out into short ridiculous giggles. I lurched to my feet and knocked away Maddie's arm. I started to stagger over to the bathroom, but went down to my knees before I could make it, and knelt there stupidly, giggling like an idiot. Maddie's lips set in a grim line. She came and hoisted me upright. 'The first time I trust you to take yourself home, what goes on? You wander off and roll in at two o'clock in the morning! How's that? Now, where have you been?'

'I've been out with Riccy Corday,' I yelped, mad as anything. 'He's a gentleman, and I've done nothing to be ashamed of. So there. And what's more, I'm leaving here — I'm not having you bossing me around as if I was a kid.'

'Riccy Corday?' Her eyebrows shot up. 'You damned little fool! Hasn't anyone ever told you about that cheapskate?'

'Yeah, I've heard things, but they don't worry me. Jealous minds always make some story up.'

'So you think the tales about him are lies?'

'I know they are. He's a perfect gentleman.'

'He didn't get fresh with you, then?'

I thought of lying for a minute, but then I knew she'd have seen seen right through me. 'Well yes, he did.'

Her fingers bunched together and she stepped forward. 'The dirty rat — and you just a kid. What happened?'

I gave her a haughty look. 'You don't think I'd let anything happen to me, do you? I told him I didn't like it, and he stopped. That proves that he's a gentleman, doesn't it?'

'It proves nothing of the sort. It only proves he wants you so badly he'd rather wait than risk losing you by rushing his fences. You mad little idiot, can't you see that?'

'No, I can't,' I told her sulkily. 'And it won't be any good you arguing with me, either. I like him — and I can take care of myself. You've taught me how. How do you know Corday doesn't feel differently about me than about the other women he's been with?'

'How d'you mean?'

I flushed a little. 'Well, he could be in love — want to even marry me!' I concluded defiantly.

'You poor little simp! Men like Corday don't marry. You'll be an attraction only as long as he doesn't get tired of you. Then he'll toss you aside and go for somebody else. I know that, and I'm swearing it to you. Believe me, I know what I'm talking about.'

'I prefer to believe my own intuition,' I told her.

'Intuition? You haven't any, kid. You're too young. It's just that he's the first handsome thing in pants who's ever tried to molest you, and you're flattered, although you wouldn't admit it, not even to yourself. But later, you'll get to know his kind. There'll be dozens of them. If I wasn't looking after you there'd have been dozens already. Maybe you'd have wound up as just one of those bodies they periodically fish up from the Hudson — I guess Riccy's been responsible for more than one of those deaths.'

I knew in my heart every word she was saying was true, but it still stung, and I stubbornly decided I'd have to make a stand for it now, or never. She wasn't going to rule *me!* I said: 'I don't care what you say — I'm seeing him tomorrow night, too.'

'You are? Then take my tip while there's time — give him a miss. You may be in burlesque now, but that doesn't mean you've got to be cheap. Far from it. Someday there'll be a nice kid for you someplace — like I thought there'd be one for me, one day, only I kinda muffed it. I'm sorry now. Don't you go doing the same over again, honey.'

I refused to be placated. 'Maybe you're jealous yourself?'

'Maybe I am — but not of Corday. I'm jealous of your youth and your freshness — so damned jealous I want you to keep it that way, and not spoil yourself, or let any two-timing rat spoil it for you. *That's* how I feel, Lucille.'

I didn't answer; I turned my head away, and she sighed. She said: 'Look at me — come on, turn your head here and up at me. That's right. What do you see?'

'I — I don't know what you mean.'

'You do, but you won't say — you don't want to hurt my feelings, do you? Well, I'll tell you, kiddo. You see a dame who's had it — and how? The lines at the corners of my peepers; the blue circles around them; the deep grooves at the ends of my mouth. Usin' artificial aids to bolster up my courage and my figure. Sure, I get by on stage under the limelights — make-up can give you a hand there. But how do I look in the mornings when I crawl out of bed, wondering where I'm gonna end up when I'm too old for the show? What have I got? No dough, and no guy who'd marry me either, not once he's seen me like I really am. I'm a good-time girl — you've heard about us. We're the life and soul of the party when we're young. We've got guys by the hundred. But when we get to about thirty-eight to forty, and start looking around for a guy to hitch up with us, funny thing is, we suddenly lose all our popularity. There *isn't* any guy for us. There never is. We get to wandering, haunting soup kitchens, and sometimes we even get lower than that — until finally there ain't any soul left at all, just a *body* — and nobody *wants* that body anymore. Nobody . . . and then it's the river.'

She was putting everything she knew into her words. For a minute I was horrified, knowing her to be right. But then that stubborn streak came up again. I turned my head towards her, looked her full in the eyes, and said: 'You still haven't convinced me that Riccy's bad for me.'

'Riccy? Sure, that punk,' she said, and her eyes clouded over. 'I knew Riccy almost fifteen years ago when I was just a kid like you — when I first started in burlesque; when I thought someday I'd have a home and a family. Sure, I knew Riccy. He was younger then, but he looked the same. And by God, he *was* the same. The same dirty, low-down, stinking warthog he is now. He likes 'em young! I found that out. He was the same way with me as he's being with you. No, no, he didn't want anything from me. If he did get fresh, it was just his admiration for my beauty carrying him away. That went on for some time — and I didn't have anyone to advise me, and I'm sure I'd have ignored them if I had.'

I still didn't speak, although her words had impressed me very deeply. I didn't know whether she was making all that about Riccy up for my benefit, but it didn't worry me. What did worry me was that I saw it could easily happen like she said. Perhaps, if she'd just driven it in a bit longer, I'd have washed Riccy out there and then, and spared myself a lot of heartache. But she didn't.

She looked at my face, then gave a sigh. 'You don't think it could happen like that to you, do you? Tell me, do you like Riccy?'

'Why, yes — very much.'

'Wouldn't some ordinary, decent boy be as much fun?'

I shook my head.

'Then promise me one thing,' she said, gripping my hand. 'I don't want you to leave here — I like you being around a lot. But just give me your word you won't put up with any funny business from that low-down skunk, and that the second he tries to get cute you'll hand him his hat and find the nearest elevator.'

That was just what I had in mind myself. I said: 'I give you my word on that, Maddie.'

'Thanks. I think a lot of you, honey. And — '

'Yes?'

'If ever you're in a jam . . . you know . . . you'll come to me, won't you?'

I nodded. All my animosity towards her had vanished now. She patted my shoulder. 'That's a good kid. Well, from here on you're a free agent. I won't try to guide you anymore — but just always remember you're only seventeen yet, huh? And that there's a whole bunch of things you still don't know. Will you do that?'

Again I nodded. She grinned then. 'An' next time you see Riccy, tell him Maddie wants to be remembered to a dirty louse — and if anything happens to you, she'll personally fix him! Now come on to bed, kid, and sleep it off.'

6

We're Closing You Down

After that one time, Maddie never bothered me about Riccy again. And Riccy was always with me. He did show me fun; I found out what it was like to go to the best night spots, to have other women gazing at me admiringly and to have swell clothes, furs and silks, and wonderful jewellery to wear. Riccy got all that for me; at first I tried to refuse his endless gifts, but he laughed and told me there weren't any strings attached to them, he didn't want a thing for them but my company, and he insisted I take them.

So I did; who wouldn't? And eventually I got hardened to taking them — in fact, I even expected them, looked forward to them — and I was never disappointed. He always had something for me. He was the most thoughtful man I had ever met. Nor did he ever try to get fresh with me again, at that time.

Maddie and I continued to room together, and forgot our past quarrel. You couldn't have held a grudge against Maddie, and when she saw I was all right with Riccy, her fears seemed to ease off a bit. And Mitzi — Mitzi Larue . . . well, I didn't know it and neither did Riccy, but there was trouble brewing!

She hated me; hated me like poison. I saw her once or twice in front, with a couple of bowler-hatted men who didn't look the usual type to visit burlesque. In fact, Tim Foley used to view these two and say: 'By God, if I didn't know Mitzi Larue, I'd say those two had something to do with morality in this town. They look like they've got a say in what the vice squad does. Like a coupla retired parsons poking their blue noses into other folks' pleasures.'

'You haven't got a thing to worry about,' said Maddie. 'Even if they *are* vice squad touts, they can't pin you down. The show's as clean as any other in town, isn't it? There's no exposure — even the strip acts like me get a quick blackout before they've really come clean. Everything's more or less under cover. So what could they do to you, Timmy boy?'

It was as she had said; one or two morality societies had been snooping around town trying to get places closed up. They'd had some luck with one or two joints, where the shows were worse than just saucy. They'd shut down several of those dumps. But taken as a burlesque show with the regulation quota of strips in it, Foley's was far cleaner than the average.

We found out how it happened later; pity we didn't have an idea that something was due to break. We might have, what with Mitzi and those two morality nosey parkers out in front. We might have guessed she was waiting for a chance to set them on to us, and we might have guessed also that if a chance didn't roll up of its own accord, she'd be the type to make one herself.

It happened to me and three more of the girls. Halfway through the last show, we used to do a little number called 'Singing in the Shower.' For this, the four of us stood behind a piece of transparent gauzy stuff that looked like frosted glass. We went through the motions of disrobing and getting under the shower while we sang our number. The audience could really only see the vague shapes of our forms through the gauze, but like most audiences they had damned fine imaginations, and were able to supply all the details themselves in their mind's eye. They loved the number, of course.

From about three inches below the hollow of our throats, we were visible above the gauze. This meant that to keep up the illusion for the customers, all we were able to wear was a pair of skin-tight trunks, and nothing above them. But that didn't count. The stagehands couldn't see us — the stage was fixed that way. The only guy who got a really fair view was the little runt up in the fly, who lowered and raised the piece of gauze we used. Only this night, just when we were clean stripped to the waist, he lowered it altogether on us, and the folks let out one yell!

We panicked a bit, and instead of

getting off stage we stood looking up and yelling for him to yank the gauze up again. But he didn't. And then, over the roar of the audience, a woman said: 'I knew we'd catch them if we waited long enough! Do your duty, gentlemen.'

The two bowler-hatted guys walked along the aisle and climbed onto the stage. Tim Foley came rushing on from one side as the four of us girls picked up the clothes we'd discarded and hastily put them on again.

One of the bowler-hats said: 'Is your name Foley?'

Tim nodded glumly.

'It is? Then I have to inform you that we're closing down this place as being lewd and obscene. You'll have a charge to answer, also.'

'But it was an accident,' wailed Tim. 'That wasn't planned to happen — believe me. The guy who jerks the scenery let us all down.'

'We aren't concerned with that,' sniffed one of the two. 'You can make any statement you have to make to the judge. Good night.'

And they blew!

We all felt pretty bad about it; and when Tim caught the little runt who'd let us down, sneaking out, there was hell to pay. He got hold of him by the collar and yanked him mid-stage. The clients had beat it now, and the theatre was closed and locked, not to reopen until the mess had been straightened out. The little runt looked a bit sick about it all, and when Foley started asking him questions he actually started blubbing!

'Come on,' grunted Tim. 'Don't tell us it was an accident. You dropped it down and left it down. Why?'

'I dud-dud-didn't,' pleaded the runt. 'Honest I didn't, boss.'

'Then what's this?' demanded Foley, fishing about five hundred bucks out of the runt's top pocket. 'How come you're walking around with five hundred smackers stuck in your pocket?'

'I — I've been saving that up. Honest, boss.'

'How long've you been saving it?'

'About ten years now, honest, boss.'

'An' you use your top breast pocket for a bank?'

'Yeah, yeah, that's it. I like to keep it on me.'

'So you just saved it a dollar or so at a time, did you?'

'Honest, boss.'

'Then how d'you account for the fact that each bill's got a *consecutive* number on it?'

That turned him. He licked his lips and whined: 'I don't know . . . Maybe I — maybe I . . . I don't know.'

'No, but I do. You took that dough from someone to sell the show out. Ain't I right?'

'No, you ain't right. I saved that dough.'

Foley sighed and shoved the wad back in the little runt's jeans. 'Beat it, before I lose my temper and let you have it.'

The runt got going. The cast wandered off to get dressed, and Maddie and Tim and me looked at each other dismally. Then Tim said: 'Anyway, we've got plenty of proof that it was an accident. I don't see how they can keep us closed down

— do you, girls?'

He'd hardly finished saying that when from the direction of the stage door, Mitzi Larue strolled towards us. She was wearing elegant furs, and her fingers were sparkling with rings. She came and joined the three of us, then gave a laugh.

'So they shut your dump down, Tim Foley?'

'Yeah, they shut it down,' growled Foley. 'And unless I'm very much mistaken, it sounded like your voice that drove 'em on to us. Was it?'

'It was,' she admitted frankly. 'Yes, I closed you down. It was also me who paid your fly-man to drop the gauze at the crucial moment. An' how do you like that?'

Foley groaned. 'What've you got against me, Miss Larue? I didn't ever do you any harm, did I?'

'I've nothing against you, Foley,' she answered, smiling. 'But for that dame there . . . ' She glared right at me. 'I hate her guts. And that's why you're closed down, Tim Foley.'

Foley knew all about me taking Riccy

from Mitzi, and now he nodded. 'I get it. You'll throw the whole company out of work just for the sake of getting back at one kid who happened to appeal to the guy you wanted and couldn't have.'

'That's it exactly. Now if you toss this floozie out on her ear, I'll see what I can do for you.'

'No thanks. No dice. This'll be cleared out when it gets to court, you'll see.'

'Sorry, Timmy.' She grinned. 'It won't be that easy for you. I've got the judge who tries these things right in my pocket. He'll do just what I say for him to do — I know too much about him.'

She wasn't joking about it, either. Tim tried a new angle. 'How about yourself? Aren't you stickin' your own neck out somethin' awful, sister?' he said. 'Your own little club ain't exactly a haunt for maiden ladies, is it? Suppose I sic 'em on to you, Mitzi?'

'Wouldn't worry me, Timmy boy. I pay for protection — the cops often drop in at my dump for a snootful of illegal booze. So you'd be wasting time. I even sell the stuff by the barrelful to the D.A. and three of the local judges.'

'Okay, so I'm tied up, am I? What's your proposition?'

'It's easy. You pitch out this cheap dame here, and I'll call off the hounds. I can do that, too. You'll be open again, and better packed out for the publicity you've had by tomorrow night. If you don't agree to that, I wager I'll see you don't ever open again here, Foley. I can fix that, you know I can.'

He knew it all right. And so did we. But, like the good guy he was, he said: 'Get out of this theatre, Mitzi. Lucille stays on here, and that's final. Nobody tells me what to do and what not to do. Now beat it before I take you by the seat of your pants and sling you out personally.'

'Then you won't beat her out?'

'She stays as long as she wants.'

'That's decent of you, Tim,' I put in, stepping forward. 'But I'd meant to pack it up anyway. I'll leave now, and then this dragon can call off her stooges. I don't want anyone suffering on my account, and if I stay we'll all be out of

74

a job. So I'll go.'

He looked at me, and I could see the gratitude in his eyes. Maddie said: 'Good for you, kiddo. And you won't ever have to worry about having someplace to stay and something to eat as long as I've got a little dough.'

'Thanks, Maddie. So as of now, Tim, I resign, and thanks for all you've done for me. It's been swell.'

7

I'll Make You a Queen!

By the time I'd cooled off and come down from the dressing rooms, ready to leave, Mitzi had already gone. She'd left vowing to see I didn't get another job in show business, and with the pull I knew she had, I was afraid she'd make good her threat.

It worried me more than you'd think. You get used to theatre life — the greasepaint gets in your nostrils, the blare of the band from the distance dins in your ears, the glare of the spotlight sticks in your eyes so that it becomes a part of you, and you're never happy unless you're up there giving out.

The thought that I might never get a spot again filled me with unimaginable misery. I wandered out of the theatre without seeing Maddie again, and found

Riccy waiting for me outside the stage door.

'Hello, kid.' He grinned. 'You're out early, aren't you? What's wrong?'

'It's Mitzi,' I told him dejectedly. 'She's used her influence to get the show closed down, and she says she'll see it stays shut down unless Tim Foley kicks me out.'

'What?' His face grew darker, and he clenched his fists. 'By God, she can't pull that stuff! You tell Tim Foley you're staying . . . I'll see what I can do about it.'

'No use, Riccy. I've already said I'd leave.'

'But kid, you shouldn't have jumped so quick. Maybe I could've fixed things for you.'

'I doubt it. Mitzi's got all the pull around here. No, I'll just have to dig around and see if I can find work somewhere else.'

'Sure, that's it. Any place'd be glad to take you — you'd be useful to any show, I know it.'

I shook my head, smiled a bit, and said: 'I'm afraid it won't be in show business, Riccy. Mitzi also said she'd take damn good care I didn't get another break in New York. The only thing to do if I want to stay in the game is to accept tours in brokendown little vaudeville dumps. And I don't like that idea.'

He looked thoughtful. 'Neither do I. That'd mean you leaving New York, honey, and that I don't want. No, I think we can do something better than that — much better. By heck, yes!'

He was getting excited suddenly. His eyes were gleaming and he was thumping one fist into the palm of the other hand. He took a long look at me, then said: 'I've been thinking you're wasted back there at Foley's for a long time. And — I've got some spare cash I want to invest in a sound proposition.'

'I don't get it, Riccy.'

'No? Well, I'll tell you. I'm going to make you a queen, Lucille! A queen of burlesque! How'd you like that?'

I laughed at him and his enthusiasm. 'You don't think I'd let you throw any money away on that, do you? Besides, it still doesn't solve the problem of who'd hire me.'

'You don't need *anyone* to hire you!' he exclaimed.

I looked at him, puzzled. I could see he had something big to spring on me, and I was beginning to get excited myself. 'But I can't work without a theatre,' I told him. 'Where'll I find a theatre to take me now?'

'You'll have your own theatre!'

I couldn't believe him for a time. But when he explained, I was as taken with the idea as he was.

'Look, honey,' he said, 'there's the Bexton Hall empty and has been ever since they quit using it as a dance hall. Okay. I step in, buy the joint up, have it redecorated, get a swell interior artist to design the whole dump, get a good company, put you in as star, and reopen it with a brand-new show. New ideas, new names, new figures. What happens?'

'You go broke,' I said skeptically.

'Baloney. The shekels roll in — we can't count 'em fast enough. And you and me split fifty-fifty, after the staff's been paid. How about it, kid? Can we make a go of it?'

'It's sounding wonderful to me right now,' I said doubtfully. 'But . . . I don't know, Riccy. You shouldn't risk all that money on me. If I was a star in my own right, yes. But I'm not. I'm a cheap third-rate leg act, and it wouldn't feel right if I didn't get there the hard way.'

'Nuts,' he said impetuously. 'To hell with the hard way. You'd have gotten there sooner or later anyhow, but Mitzi took the chance off you. So here's where we get on back at Mitzi.'

'And suppose she tried closing the Bexton down?'

His face darkened again. 'She'd have a damn sight more sense than to meddle with anything I was running. If she did get funny, something very unpleasant would happen.'

'You really mean all this, Riccy?'

'Sure I do. You know a whole lot about burlesque now. You got a fair idea of what the customers want, haven't you? You could arrange it all if I signed the cheques, couldn't you?'

'I — I don't know. You mean me to handle the whole thing? Even to having the theatre done up?'

'That's the notion. You could do it?'

'I'd like some — some help. I'd like someone more experienced to guide me. A girl friend, for instance.'

'Who? Name anyone you want.'

'It'd be hard to get her to leave the job she has now. She's starring at Foley's — I mean Maddie . . . '

'Maddie? Maddie Maritza?'

'Yes — I think you used to know her, didn't you?'

'Er, why, sure. I did know her once, just as a casual sort of friend. Isn't there anyone else who'd do?'

I shook my head. 'No, I wouldn't like to risk a thing like this without a clever head to guide me. Maddie's got the whole racket at her fingertips — and on top of that I owe her a lot.'

'I see. Well, okay, kid, if you want her. I won't say I approve, but it's your theatre. You hire whoever you like — and don't worry about the salary. I'll take care of that.'

'Thanks, Riccy,' I told him, and impulsively I got hold of his lapels and kissed him — I was getting very fond of him by then.

I told Maddie about my plans that night. She didn't say anything about Riccy, but she did say: 'It's a big break for you, baby. But promise me you'll take care of yourself, huh? Promise me that. You won't have anyone to look after you over there . . . '

'But I will, Maddie,' I told her. 'I'll have you.'

'*Me*?'

'Certainly. You don't think I'd take a job on like this if I didn't have someone clever behind me, do you?'

'But kid, I'm working with Foley.'

'For how long?'

She grinned. 'You're right, I am getting past it. I bet he'll give me the push anyway before next year. Make room for some girl who doesn't have to go through hell tryin' to keep down her figure.'

'That's what I mean. Why wait for the thin end of the wedge? Make a break now — and co-star with me at the new Bexton.'

'Co-star? No, sir. Riccy said you're

gonna be the star of this show, and what chance would I have to shine against you, anyway? Why, the guys at Foley's thought a hell of a lot more of you than they did of me, and me the star at that. No, I wouldn't co-star at all.'

'But Maddie . . . '

'Now don't argue. I'm getting past it anyway. Why should you have an old hag in your show, just because you happen to know me?'

She was determined; I'd seen her that way before and knew it was useless to argue. So I sprang a surprise I'd thought up just in case she cut up like this about things. 'All right, so you won't be in the show. But we need you. And there's one spot where you don't have to worry about growing old. I know you'd show everybody else what's what if you'd do it.'

'What's up your sleeve, honey?'

'I want you to be my producer and manager. You've had years in burlesque, and you know it inside and out. I couldn't get anyone finer than you for the job. Say you'll take it, Maddie. Please?'

'Honey,' she said, standing up and

coming over, 'you know darned well I can't refuse an offer like that, don't you? But how about Riccy? He won't like it.'

'He doesn't mind a bit. I've told him I need you.'

'Maybe you think he doesn't mind, but he does underneath.'

'But why should he?'

She shrugged. 'I dunno. Maybe he's got designs on you and is scared I'll jam a spoke into his wheel.'

'Would you, Maddie?'

'I sure would.'

'Then I need you more than ever to look after me. You must come, please.'

She gripped my arm, and I wouldn't swear to it, but I think I saw a tear glinting in the old battle-axe's eye. She said huskily: 'Sure I will. Let Riccy think what he likes. You're the best friend I ever had, kid, and I mean to see you don't come to no harm from any well-dressed wolves. I'll take the job — and thanks, kid. Maybe you've saved me from the river, after all.'

* * *

Riccy bought the Bexton the very next day. He had workmen on the job within a week, and the old dance hall rapidly underwent a startling change. He spent money in the most reckless and extravagant manner, and paid no attention to my remonstrations. He had the floor above the theatre converted into a suite of luxurious rooms especially for my use. A fortune was spent on advertising alone. All of New York knew the old Bexton Hall was reopening under the name of the Bexton Burlesque Theatre.

It was Maddie's idea for me to change my name. Lucille Barry wouldn't do for a burlesque queen, she said. It'd have to have more snap, more naughtiness about it — something cuddly for the boys to call me by. Eventually she decided on 'Cutie.' And when the grand opening was announced, I was billed in three-foot letters all over town, as the great French star direct from the Folies Bergere — Lucille 'Cutie' Dubarry! If you remember me at all, that's the name you'll remember me by, I expect. Anyway, that's the name I had when I ran into all my trouble.

Maddie was invaluable; I never could have pulled it off without her. She was producer, talent scout, dance director, stage manager, and every darned thing I could think of. She personally was determined to see me hit the top. She was convinced I wasn't going to stay being a burlesque star all my life. Someday, she told me, they'd clamour for me on Broadway — and although I thought this was hardly likely, I decided to do my best to live up to her hopes for me.

Funny thing about Maddie; she was almost like a mother to me. I think that was really what was at the back of her kindness. She wouldn't have admitted it even, but she had a strong maternal instinct for all her rough way of life — and I couldn't forget that night when she'd told me how she'd hoped one day for a decent husband and kids of her own.

She picked the entire show, selected the dance routines and staged them, and chose the songs. She devised new and original ideas that were sure to attract a vast crowd, and rehearsed us all until the sweat ran from us, and then made us do it all again. She hand-picked the chorus girls and showgirls. There were twenty of them, straight-legged, wide-hipped. Ideal for any show, and the tired businessman's delight. What was more, they were all *decent* girls.

There's an impression abroad — even today — that chorus girls, and theatre folk in general, are, let's say, uninhibited. That's a lie — a downright lie! Just because one star makes herself notorious to attract the public eye doesn't say all do. I can tell you that showgirls are not only as decent, morally, as other folks — they're even more decent, most of them. But newspapers love any scandal attached to theatre folk — it's big news. And when anything does go wrong, the respectable city man reads it out to his wife:

'Listen, dear — says here: 'Wild party bust up by police. Six showgirls arrested.' My, my, those *theatre* people. It's disgusting. Thank God *we* all live a normal, straightforward life!'

The trouble is, they should get wise to

themselves. But usually it's the worst of them who have the most to say about what a low lot actresses are. The husband always cracks that, just before he goes out to hang around some stage door to hit on the girl who was third from the left in the front row of the chorus — the one who smiled at him as he sat in the stalls. Hypocrites, all of them!

8

Queen of Burlesque

It was a wonderful opening. Lots of people who *were somebody* around town came along, and the whole company gave the show of its life. I was a riot, even if I say it myself. But I don't take any credit for my success — no, that's all due to Maddie and Riccy. I supplied the figure and the face, but it was Riccy who gave me the chance, and Maddie who picked my numbers and staged my routines.

And there was Mitzi Larue, with an awful glare on her face, right in the front row. While the audience were holding up the show yelling for me to do an encore, I sneered right in her face. I couldn't resist it.

She hissed at me, heedless of the people listening: 'You wait, you cheap bitch! You think because Riccy's carrying a glow for you that I won't try and get under your feet again. But you're wrong, dead wrong. Just wait!'

But I was too full of my reception as a fully-fledged queen of burlesque to give a hang what she said. I felt sure she couldn't do anything now — so sure that I didn't even worry about her anymore.

Which was where I made my big mistake.

Riccy came round to see me after the show — he'd been in a business conference someplace and hadn't been able to attend the opening. But he came around and called on me in the rooms above the theatre which he'd had specially built.

'Hear you were a riot, baby,' he said. 'It's all over town what a hit you made. The joint's booked up for months in advance. I told you, didn't I, that we'd clean up?'

'It wasn't me, Riccy,' I pleaded. 'It was really Maddie — she worked awfully hard to put it over.'

'Oh, sure, Maddie,' he said, not too enthusiastic. 'Sure, she did her bit, didn't she? Well, you're the boss — give her a raise if you think she deserves it, and forget her.' He slumped down onto the couch and patted the place next to him. Maybe I didn't know him as well as I thought, though; for as his eyes lit on one of my legs poking out of the front of my gown, he pulled me against him roughly.

'Please, Riccy,' I protested. 'Don't do that. Don't spoil it all now.'

'But listen, kid, I won't hurt you any. I've played along and been patient — I've fixed this show up for you — hell, what else do I have to do?'

I opened my eyes wide and stared at him. 'Riccy! You don't mean you did all this to — '

I could see he was in an unreasonable frame of mind. Now I was regretting accepting his offer of doing all this for me. I might have known there'd be something behind it.

'Sure,' he agreed. 'Why'd you think I fixed up this suite of rooms here, only for you an' me to be alone together, baby?'

I stood up, hardly knowing what to say.

'Don't give me that hurt line, kid. Why not play ball? I've done plenty for you, and I'd kind of thought you were getting to like me a lot, too.'

'I am, Riccy, honest I am. But — you don't understand me yet. You see — you know . . . ' I tried desperately to think of some way to put it, but couldn't.

Maddie saved me the effort. She came in from the bathroom at that moment and said: 'Hello? I thought I heard the big bad wolf's dulcet tones in here. I'll tell you why she doesn't want any of your truck, Riccy my bucko. Because she happens to be a good girl and wants to *stay* that way until some guy's big enough to marry her.'

Riccy had got up with an awful scowl. He now growled: 'What's this hard-faced dame doing here, Lucille?'

'I've been grabbing myself a bath,' she told him, speaking for me.

'Yeah? And hasn't your own hotel room got a bathroom?'

'I haven't got any hotel room. I'm staying here, Romeo.'

Riccy turned to me questioningly.

'That's true, Riccy. Oh, don't be angry with me. I couldn't live up here myself all alone. I asked Maddie to stay with me.'

'That's so,' Maddie confirmed. 'I didn't think being alone would hurt her — long as she *stayed* all alone. But I got an idea I might be needed to keep the big bad wolf from the door. Seems I was.'

Riccy snarled, his face black with temper. 'Damn you, Lucille. Do you have to tote this wet nurse everywhere with you? Can't you look after yourself? You must've known I fixed this suite for you and me.'

'No, I didn't know that, Riccy,' I told him stonily. 'Nor would I ever have consented if I had. I don't want it that way, ever. I do think the world of you, but I'm not being played around with. If you want me so badly, you can ask me to marry you.'

'And what about the dough I've given away to fix you up with this joint? Doesn't that count?'

Maddie butted in with: 'This place is a goldmine. You'll have back every cent you ever spent within a few months, and you know it. So Lucille doesn't owe you a thing, smarty.'

'You damned well stay out of this,' hissed Riccy. He whipped back to me. 'All right. But I'm telling you — get this old has-been out of here by tomorrow night, or else.' He slammed on his hat, turned on his heel, and stalked from the room, leaving me gazing after him, very near to blubbering.

Maddie came over and put her arm around me. She whispered: 'Don't worry over it, honey.'

'I — I can't help it,' I almost sobbed. 'I was really getting to love him a lot, Maddie. Oh, why did he have to go and spoil it all like this? If he'd only gone about it the right way, I might even have lived with him — but he was horrible.'

'Then I'm glad he was, Cutie,' she said softly. 'Because you aren't the type to go off with any guy like that. I knew why he'd had this suite arranged up here — I can read him like a book. Up until now you've seen only the cover — and it's pretty elegant. But inside, the book's plain rotten. A travesty and a mockery of life, kid, without any decency or humanity in it from start to end. That's Riccy inside.' She grinned. 'Say — I'm spouting like a blessed poet, ain't I? I never thought I even knew words like that 'til just a moment ago. Maybe I ought to be a book-writer myself. I reckon if I was, they'd ban 'em in Boston — they sure would.' She smoothed back my hair, adding: 'Snap to, baby. Don't let a lug like that upset you.'

I took her advice; it was always good, even if oddly put.

Maddie stayed on; and Riccy, in a temper, stayed away. I got so I didn't mind him not coming around anymore — the only time I ever saw him was down in the office when we reckoned up and split the takings every Saturday night. My life was getting too full to mind missing Riccy much. I was asked most every night to some late party, and I usually went. Dates were eagerly sought from me, and I accepted several — but always I took Maddie and one of her boyfriends with me.

The year ran out and it got well into February of the following year. If I'd stopped to think, I might have realised I wasn't as happy as I should have been. I wasn't getting the fun I should have had. Oh, I was getting my share of what the socialites like to call fun — cocktail parties, late-night dancing, supper clubs, swell dinners, and lots and lots of lovely clothes and jewellery. But now I was hankering after another kind of fun — the kind I used to have with a boy I liked back home — Sunday picnics and weenie roasts and sails down the river, just the two of us together, talking about what we were going to make of the future and how we would never part. Kids' stuff, yes; but it was the stuff that makes for happiness and contentment.

There was too much glitter about my present life. Hardly a day passed without some snoopy photographer grabbing a pic of me climbing out of an automobile with a high step, or changing in my dressing room backstage. You couldn't hold these guys; they had to secure stuff for the mags they worked on. And just when I least thought any of them would be around, they'd suddenly whip up from nowhere and grab a close-up of me adjusting my suspender. That kind of thing gets monotonous; but as a toasted queen of burlesque, and a strip artiste second to none, I had to take it.

Months rolled by without Riccy ever trying to crash in on me again; until one night, when I'd left Maddie at a party and gone home very tired, he was sitting there when I walked in.

'Riccy!'

'Hiya, kiddo. Thought I'd drop in, baby.'

'I'm glad you did. It's been a long time. I'll get you a drink — '

'Hold it; I got one myself. Poured one for you, too. Where's prune-face?'

He meant Maddie by that; was probably referring to the wrinkles she was collecting on her face. She'd been living more riotously than ever since she'd quit the boards — maybe she knew she wouldn't reign very long now and was making the most of it.

'She's still partying,' I said.

He looked pleased at that. 'Good — then it's me and you alone, huh?'

'Riccy, you aren't meaning to suggest anything again?'

'No, no, Cutie. I've forgotten all about that. Here, have your drink and let's talk it over. I came by here to see if you'd still be interested in that proposition of marriage I made to you.'

'You never made me any, Riccy.'

'I didn't? No, that's right. Well, I'm making it now. How about it, sweets?'

I sipped my drink. 'I don't know. Can I think it over?'

'Sure, take as long as you like. I can wait — waited a long time already.'

He poured me more liquor, and I sipped thoughtfully. I didn't know what to make of his change of heart — didn't know if it was quite genuine. He didn't seem genuine to me, but then, he never did. He was off-handed about the biggest things, Riccy.

I began to feel funny in the head. That was surprising. I'd grown used to drink by now, and I hadn't taken much that night. But I was suddenly light and giggly, and awfully weak. I saw Riccy looking at me sideways with a funny sort of grin on his face. A sudden suspicion grew in my mind, and I turned feebly to stare into his eyes.

'Riccy,' I mumbled, 'what — what have you — done? I — I feel awful.'

'Don't fret yourself, Cutie. Just a little pick-up in your drink. You needed it — you're clean worn out. Make you feel good.'

I felt my head whirling; I began to slide towards him, unable to hold upright. I heard him chuckle, felt him lift me in his arms, and then everything went black.

Slowly I came back to consciousness. Maddie stood in the doorway. She held a small gun in her hand. I didn't even know she possessed one, but by the look of her she knew quite well how to use it. Her face was cold, as if carved from grey stone. Her eyes were hard and glassy. She grated: 'I was expecting something like this.'

Riccy was afraid of her, but grunted: 'Why don't you go throw yourself from the roof? It's all over between us anyway.'

'Not for you it isn't — I can make you suffer, you punk.'

'What do you mean by that?' he hissed, eyes narrowing.

'You'll see. *Get going!*' She watched him put his overcoat on, then followed him to the door. When she came back, I was sobbing my heart out.

9

Riccy Gets Out

She came over after she'd made coffee, and made me drink a cup. She gripped my arm and said: 'Now don't go upsetting yourself, baby. There wasn't a thing you could've done about it anyway.'

'There was, Maddie. If only I'd taken your advice and steered clear of Riccy.'

Her lips were set grimly. 'Don't worry, honey. He won't be around to bother you anymore.'

I remembered the gun she carried. I said, frightened: 'Maddie — you — you wouldn't . . . ?'

'Murder him? Sure I would, if I thought I could get away with it. But I couldn't, and I ain't got the least intention of frying for that low skunk. No, I'll just make this town too hot to hold him, that's all.'

'But how?'

'Never mind how. I got methods.'

She wouldn't say any more than that. But knowing her as I did, I knew she wasn't shooting any line, and that she had something on Riccy that would send him out of town before you'd have time to bust a brassiere strap by inhaling a deep breath!

★ ★ ★

I was right at that; it was only a night later when, taking the air outside the theatre alone, I was yanked into the shadows by a guy with a dark coat on, upturned collar, and trilby hauled down over his pan. He clapped a hand over my mouth, dragged me into the shadows and muttered: 'Keep *quiet*. It's me, Riccy.'

'Riccy? What . . . ?'

'*I'll* tell you *what*,' he said viciously. 'I'm on the run — I'm hightailing it out of town, along to Pittsburgh.'

'But why?'

'The cops are on my trail. Maybe you know my racket, and you also probably know there's one or two things I go in for besides pin-tables and booze. Well, that damned fish-faced friend of yours has dug up one or two little details that have made the cops very anxious to see me. They've already roped in Barney and Sharkey, two of my boys. Luckily, Al happened to get wind about the rake-in, and he was able to get clear and give me the tip they were after us. So now Al and me are blowing Pittsburgh way, thanks to that damned meddling female you think's your friend. That's what she meant when she said she'd get back at me, see?'

I didn't know what to say; I did think Maddie had gone a bit far in stooling on Riccy. So I didn't say anything.

He went on: 'Here's what I want you to do, kid. First of all, don't say a thing about where I've blown to. If you do, I'll know, and it'll go hard with you. Second, tell that blasted Maddie floozie that I'll be back when things have blown over — and tell her I'll have a word to say to her, only I'll do all my talking from the open end of a gun!'

'Riccy . . . ' I started to gasp.

'Quiet. I haven't got time to argue.

Third thing for you to latch onto is this: Come next Saturday, I want you to be outside the front of the Hotel Egremont in Pittsburgh, at nine at night.'

'Why?'

'Because I'm taking you out to a hideaway I've got in the hill country. You're sticking there with me, see. Leave word you're going to see your folks if anyone gets nosey. And no tricks, or I'll fix you as well as Maddie. Get me?'

'Suppose I refuse to do anything you ask?'

He gripped my arm so tight I could have screamed with pain. 'You better not — or maybe I'll think it over and make an end of you right here and now.'

I shuddered, knowing by his face that he was capable of it.

'Well?'

'I'll do as you say, Riccy. You've been good to me.'

'Atta girl. I knew you would. Now I have to get out of town, but quick. Don't forget — Egremont Hotel, nine Saturday next. And just in case you tote any cops along with you, I'll be very careful before

I approach you. Now — so long, kid.' He pulled me to him and gave me a kiss from which I did my best not to recoil. Then he was gone in the darkness, leaving me there numbed and petrified, unable to think straight.

I walked in, dragging my feet, dreadfully afraid for Maddie, and a bit scared for myself. I'd heard about Riccy more than once — I knew he was as hard as a rock when it served his purpose. And I wondered how Maddie and I were to get out of the jam we were in.

I still hadn't thought of anything when I reached the suite. Maddie didn't arrive in until a lot later, and when she did I told her at once what had happened.

'I've seen Riccy,' I said.

She threw off her coat hat, lit a smoke, and sat down beside me. 'I'll bet that guy had his roller skates on, huh?'

'Sort of. He was leaving in a hurry, I know. And he told me to tell you he'd be back! Back to get you. Oh, Maddie, why did you ever give him away to the police?'

She sighed. 'I'd been thinking about it for a time, kiddo. When I was kicking around with the louse, I found out all about his white slave racket and the Chinese women he's smuggled into the country. I'd often thought of putting a spoke in his wheel there. I knew the addresses of two of the places — a guy called Barney ran one for him, and a stooge called Sharkey ran the other. All I did was tip off the cops about those joints, and who I thought was at the head of them. I'm darned sorry he got to know he was hot before they'd grabbed him. But don't worry, they'll get hold of him, I'm sure. He can't escape forever, and smuggling illegal aliens into the States is a federal offence, so the feds'll be after him too. One way or another, I don't see how he can dodge 'em. Did he say where he was blowing to?'

What was I to say to that? I felt I just couldn't give Riccy away so easily, so carelessly. He had done a lot for me — even if he had expected a lot in return. No, I couldn't play stool-pigeon easily. I don't know where I got my sense of loyalty from, but with me a confidence has always stayed a confidence; that's why

I couldn't tell her.

'No, he didn't say.'

She gave me a keen glance. 'If you say so, Lucille. But don't worry yourself over him — he wasn't any good, and whenever you get to wondering about him just remember what he pulled on you.'

And that was that; there wasn't any further sense in talking or arguing. If Riccy wasn't caught, it was a sure thing someday he'd be back to get Maddie. And me. One thing I did know, and that was that I wasn't going out to him. Nothing could have made me! He'd keep that date outside the Egremont in Pitts all on his lonesome!

There didn't seem much sense in closing down the Bexton Theatre either, not now we were doing so well. Riccy's disappearance just meant there was a bigger cut for me, and I split it fairly with Maddie.

They didn't get Riccy; months rolled on, and by and by I'd almost managed to wipe him right out of mind. But not entirely. I still used to wonder where he was, and if the heat was still on, and often

I'd hear a sound in the night in the shadows, and my heart would jump right out of my mouth, in anticipation of feeling hot lead spurt into my body. Meanwhile I carried on at the Bexton — the show was still packing 'em in. The Bexton, you'll remember, had become a showplace of New York. Country yokels in town on a jag always made for there to see the Queen of New York Burlesque, Cutie Dubarry — me.

As time went on and I didn't hear anything more from Mitzi Larue about anything, I got more careless. Since that incident in the bedroom with Riccy, too, I didn't care much what I did.

The morality societies had more or less shut up shop in response to popular derision by the public, and for the time being the twenties really were roaring. Every morning newspaper carried details of some new atrocities: gang warfare, fifteen murdered by chopper in restaurant; Dutch Schultz was doing his stuff all over the country; white slavery hit a new high, and houses of vice were littered all around the city, classy joints even having opened up on Park Avenue. Bootleggers were selling stuff hand over fist, hijacking rival gangs' consignments on the road, and beating up bartenders and saloon owners who refused to buy from them.

The country was running alive with bums; preachers were getting on their hind legs every Sunday and shooting their mouths off about heaven exacting a terrible toll for the wantonness that lay like a shroud over the city. Some of them even got personal about the gang bosses, and were later discovered floating down-river, on a one-way ticket to the heaven they seemed to love so much.

Apart from chewing gum, the cops didn't seem to do so much. They were getting big rake-offs for lying low. The gang bosses had the control of voters in various sections of the city. It paid the big-time politicians to get along with them — and if, to get along, they had to pull a string or two and get the force to lay off the gangs, they didn't mind doing that even. It wasn't as if the boss boys were convicted even when they'd been arrested and indicted. No, there was always some crooked lawyer to wriggle around the evidence; there were always two dozen apparently honest citizens to swear the big guy had been playing pool with them all night when the deed had been done.

And in the centre of it all, the Bexton Burlesque flourished and grew fat. Nobody knew then what J. Edgar Hoover was going to do to the rackets very shortly. If they had, they wouldn't have been so pleasure-mad. They'd have spent their time putting their affairs in order and making wills before the G guys really got going. But not knowing, they crowded the pool halls, gambling dens, and theatres.

As Maddie said to me: 'It's a vice boom, kiddo. But it'll end up the way they always end up. Sooner or later decent folks'll demand action — sooner or later a guy'll happen along who's big and important, and courageous enough to get after these hoodlums without worrying about what happens to himself. And then there'll be hell to pay!'

Mitzi Larue was big-time now. She had

a hand in most things that went on, and was exacting protection dough from smaller gang leaders. She was feared and hated all over town, as were her bunch of hoods — hand-picked murderers, every one of them. She was suspected of being behind several snatch jobs, but she was hand-in-hand with the police officials, and they couldn't — or maybe they wouldn't — pin her down with any charge.

My meeting with her was accidental; it happened one night when Maddie and I had gone to a late night party we'd been asked to. It was one of those wild parties down in Greenwich Village where hooch is a buck a gallon and dames a dime a dozen. There were all kinds of folk there: out-of-work actors with bow ties or cravats; starving artists without the price of a hamburger; musicians, some bums, and some of Tin Pan Alley's finest boys; racketeers of each and every description; tradesmen; street sweepers and what have you.

Maddie joined in the fun; it wasn't so long before she was sitting on top the piano singing a song she never learned at her mother's knee. A big fat so-called author was sitting with her, and a thin lanky guy dressed like Tom Mix stood behind her. I didn't really go for that kind of thing. I found myself a nice quiet would-be poet, with long hair and horn-rimmed glasses and a pained expression. He took me out onto the steps at the top of the landing to read me some of his stuff. He looked an innocent kind of sap, and I prepared myself for an hour or two of boredom.

'This is a little thing I dashed off back home in England,' he told me modestly. 'Quite tame compared to my later stuff. I'll give you the first verse,' and then he proceeded to do so. 'Like it?'

'Well,' I gasped. 'I have to admit I didn't think you had it in you. It's not so hot as poetry, but otherwise it's very hot.'

'A mere bagatelle,' he said modestly, trying to go places with his hand. 'It's very tame indeed. Now let me read you my latest one.'

'No, thanks,' I told him hastily. 'I guess your first was good enough for me, sonny. And by the way, take your hand from around my waist, will you? I thought Englishmen were gentlemen?'

'Not poets,' he told me, and laughed. We got up, and I gave him a slight push, playfully. He returned it. I lurched backward on the stairs, and he yelled: 'Look out!' But too late; when I turned, Mitzi Larue, who'd been walking up, was crashing down again from the impact of my body against hers while she'd been off balance!

And she wasn't bouncing, either!

10

Beat Up!

As she pitched backwards down the staircase, the two ugly guys walking just behind her stepped aside and watched her crash to the bottom in a flurry of arms and legs. She lay spread-eagled there, dazedly, in a most inelegant position.

My poet — my punk poet — leaned over the rails, looked down at the show, and grinned when he spotted her disarray. 'My God,' he exclaimed. ' 'Mighty oaks from little acorns grow!' Har, har!'

'Shut up, you fool,' I whispered. 'That woman's one of the biggest gang bosses around here. If she hears you, she'll have things done to you.'

He gazed at her with renewed interest. She had looked up, and her eyes went icy as they lighted on me. The two pug-uglies went down and hoisted her, somewhat breathlessly, to her dogs again. She had gone rather fat since the days when Riccy had been her big moment, and she knew it, I think, and didn't like the idea at all. Now she grunted at her stooges: 'You pair of lopsided illegitimates! Why didn't you catch me when I fell?'

'I'd sooner get in the way of the Chicago express train,' the bigger of them told her.

His buddy said: 'Sure, that's so, Mitzi. My name ain't Sampson neither. You ain't no fairy now.'

She didn't seem to resent their familiarity; maybe they knew too much about her for her to act tough with them. She took their cracks with a scowl, then ignoring them, started off up the stairs again, with the mugs trailing behind her like a couple of faithful hounds.

She stopped right in front of me and stared at me. I stared back. In the ordinary way I'd have apologised at once; but not to Mitzi. I knew there was an insult on the way, and I certainly wasn't going to humble myself then be insulted in the bargain. I waited.

'You did that on purpose,' she grated between her false snappers. 'You cheap — '

'Don't say that word again,' I begged. 'I'm tired of hearing it. Didn't they ever teach you any other cuss words at the school you attended? Or am I wrong in thinking you ever attended school? Was it reform school?'

She went from red to white; her two mugs were grinning in back of her, enjoying seeing her get slated. She snarled: 'I said you did that on purpose.'

My poet, bless him, stepped forward and said: 'She didn't. I pushed her.'

'Stay out of this, you.'

'To hell with that. I'm saying I pushed her, and what do you want to make of it, you gyrating bowl of Jell-O?'

It wasn't the first time I'd noticed a tendency to rudeness on the part of this poetic self-styled Englishman. Maybe he liked to think he was a rugged individualist — a kind of second Doctor Johnson. Whatever it was, he'd gone one too far this time with his crack. She just nodded to one of the two big birds behind her, and the next minute a ham-like fist whacked across the ear of Gabrielle Patterbury Mitt, and he lit on the floor about ten yards along the landing, and began to compose sonnets in his subconscious as like as not.

Having thus disposed of what she apparently regarded as one of nature's hardly noticeable pests, Mitzi turned her eyes on me again. 'I still say you did that on purpose. What are you doing here, anyway?'

'I was asked to a party. So what?'

'Who asked you?'

'The guy who's throwing it.'

'Then I'll step right in and have you tossed out again on your ear. He's a good friend of mine. That's where I'm going myself.'

'Don't bother,' I told her scornfully. 'It's stuffy in there already — when you get in, the atmosphere's liable to be overpowering. I don't think I could take it; I always was allergic to the smell of *skunk*!'

For about five seconds she seemed in danger of exploding. Then she snorted through her nostrils, blowing a large bubble which rather spoiled her threatening aspect. 'All right, smart dame. All right. I still owe you something about Riccy yet. I guess you was in on the plot to stool on him, too. Maybe you'll collect dividends sooner than you think.'

'From who?'

She let her eyes slide over to her uglies. I scoffed: 'They wouldn't dare touch me.'

Her eyes narrowed. 'Think so?'

I gave her a last amused glance, but I was far from feeling amused. I wanted to get away from the menace of her eyes before I showed how really scared I was. I wanted to get out of there and back home where Maddie's little gun was lying.

The mugs stepped aside as I pushed onto the stairs past them. Mitzi stood staring after me; I could see her standing there as I rounded the first bend. As I lost sight of her, she was speaking to the mugs, who were nodding knowingly.

I came onto the street and started looking for a cab. There wasn't one in sight. It was a fairly quiet street off the main stem, and not many people were around. The lighting was wicked, and the moon was just a feeble cloud-haggard glow in the heavens.

I started walking, quick; I was sorry now I hadn't chanced her having me tossed out on my ear, and gone back into the party.

I knew the mugs were following me the minute I heard the soft shuffle of feet behind. I quickened my pace and stole a look back.

Yes, there they were, dead on my tail. Hell, now I was in a fix. I began a jerky run for the main stem about fifty yards from where I was. The steps to my rear quickened too; they gained, for my evening gown impeded me from running properly. I felt their heavy breathing behind me and gave a little shriek as a large hand touched my arm. Then a thick arm circled my neck, my breathing was cut off, and I was unable to make a sound.

I tore and scratched at the hairy wrist about my neck; then the other thug gripped my hands tight and forced them downwards. He took from his pocket a length of rope and hitched my wrists tight. That done, he grabbed the hem of my gown, tore a square lump from it, and stuffed it in my mouth. A passer-by, opposite, gazed across towards us in the shadows. He gazed for about a minute — then suddenly realised what was going on, and ran like hell. No, I knew he hadn't gone for the cops — he was just putting his own precious carcass out of any harm's way.

I choked over the gag in my mouth, trying to spit it out. The smaller thug unfastened my silver belt from my flame-coloured gown and used it to fasten the gag in place. Then they pulled and pushed me along the road, past the house we'd come from, and into a narrow alleyway.

Mitzi was waiting here; her face was a mask of venom in the dim moon glow. Her eyes surveyed me frighteningly. 'Good work, boys. Hold her against the wall.'

They shoved me against it; my eyes were popping out, my teeth clenching into the material in my mouth. I could see by the look in Mitzi's eyes that she was going to be hard; too hard. Perhaps — perhaps she would even go as far as — as killing me!

I thought again and knew she wouldn't do that. The poet, when he came to, could say I'd last been seen with Mitzi and her boys. If I was found dead, that might be one rap she couldn't square with the cops, because in a way I myself was a pretty important person in the theatre world.

Then what *was* she going to do? I shivered . . .

11

Emergency Ward

I was somewhere I didn't ever remember being before. It was pitch black, and I couldn't see a thing anywhere about me. I seemed to be floating, without any physical body at all, in a void. Far off, echoing sounds rose all round me in the gloom — voices calling, like the ghostly echo of an actor's voice in an empty theatre.

There was Riccy's voice amongst them. He was saying: 'Why'd you think I fixed this suite up, baby? Why'd you think I fixed this suite up, baby? Why'd you think I fixed this suite up, baby?' on and on and on until I felt I would go mad. Then another voice cut across his, stronger, higher — Maddie!

'He's a louse, kid. Riccy's a louse, kid. He's a bad lot — a bad lot — bad lot . . . '

I suddenly found the power to scream. The sound of my own shattered voice shrilled into my ears — and then I felt a soft hand across my brow, and a masculine voice said: 'You're okay. Take it easy. You're safe here — try and sleep . . . '

I forced my eyes apart. There was a white-coated hospital intern standing over me, soothing me. I was lying in a spotlessly clean bed, in a long green-lighted ward. A nurse was standing near me with something in a glass.

The intern said: 'All right, nurse. Give her the sedative.'

I drank the stuff she offered greedily; my throat and tongue felt dry and parched. Then, without even knowing I was going to, my head slid back on the pillow and I slept again.

The next time I woke, the sun was streaming in at the window, forming patches of shadow on the polished ward floor. Nurses were bustling about the beds, and several of the other patients were standing up by the windows or propped up in bed reading. I managed to sit up and look around, and a young fair-haired nurse came hurrying over.

'Don't excite yourself, please,' she said.

'But — but — where am I, exactly? How long have I been here?'

'This is your second day. You've been in pretty bad shape, but now your condition's improving satisfactorily.'

'What — what's wrong with me?'

'Shock, mainly. But you've suffered some rather nasty injuries.'

I raised my hand and felt my face. It was a mass of bandages up to the nostrils, almost. It was sore, stiff, aching. There was something hard against my jaws. I said: 'What's wrong with my jaw, nurse?'

She frowned and looked at me dubiously. 'Your jaw was badly fractured. But don't worry about it, it's all right now.'

I could feel tight bandages around my stomach. 'And here?'

'That isn't anything to worry about. A number of superficial cuts — they'll leave scars, but they won't be noticed, of course.'

'But they will,' I said miserably. 'I'm

— I'm in burlesque.'

She forced my head back to the pillow. 'Do you feel up to talking to the police now?'

'Police?'

'Yes; this is the emergency hospital. You were picked up by a patrolman and brought here two nights ago. They've been haunting the place ever since to ask you how it all happened. There's a man outside waiting now . . . and, oh, yes. Your friend, a Miss Maritza, has been in once or twice to see you. She said she'd come back later today and see if you were conscious again.'

'You found out my name and address?'

'Yes, we found that out. It was stitched on the inside of your gown.'

I dropped back to the bed. 'I feel all right. You can ask the policeman to step in if you will, nurse.'

She nodded and went away, but returned shortly with a police sergeant. He took a chair beside the bed and took out his notebook. 'You had a pretty nasty mauling, lady, didn't you?' I nodded. 'Well, we'll get hold of the runts who did it. Just tell us all you can, huh? Know who they were?'

'No, I'm sorry.'

'So'm I. Maybe you can give a description, eh?'

I shook my head. He grunted and said: 'You aren't very helpful. You must've seen the guys.'

'I didn't. I was — was attacked from behind.'

'Hm. You sure? Or are you *scared* of sayin' who did it? Is it that?'

'No,' I lied. 'It — it isn't that at all. I just didn't see anyone.'

He snapped his notebook shut. 'Maybe you don't appreciate how bad you're hurt. Maybe if I told you, you'd feel more like coming out with the truth. They didn't tell you your looks have gone for life, did they? They didn't tell you how bad your face had been smashed up?'

I shuddered. 'No, they didn't. But — but I can guess how bad. I can feel it.'

'And you still won't talk about things?'

'I didn't see anyone.'

'Okay.' He put his book away and stood

up. 'You'll have a visit from a headquarters man shortly. Maybe he'll change your mind about getting the mob that did this. You sure must be plenty scared of someone to let a thing like this pass.' He shook his head at me, turned, and walked down the ward.

The nurse came back again, smiled at me, and gave me a drink. I said: 'Nurse, how long will I have to stay in here?'

She considered, then said: 'I can't really be sure. You'd better ask the doctor when he comes this afternoon.'

Maddie paid a visit before the doctor did. I could see her eyes were red and raw where she'd been crying. She knew I'd seen that, and sniffed: 'Don't kid yourself, honey. I've been peelin' onions, that's all. How are you, Lucille?'

I told her I felt a lot better; then she asked me how it'd happened, who'd done it. I told her that too, and her eyes blazed. She snapped: 'I'll get the cops after her and those two mugs of hers right now — I'll — '

'No, don't, Maddie — for my sake,' I pleaded. 'There's been a sergeant here trying to get information from me, but I told him nothing.'

'But honey . . . '

'I'm scared, Maddie. Even if I accused her, we couldn't make the charge stick — and she's still got boys outside who'd take care I never reached the witness stand. If I take it, she won't bother me anymore. If I kick, she'll get me.'

'It sure is a bum state when they can do things like this and get away with it. We're missing you plenty at the Bexton — when you getting out of this pre-burial factory?'

I shook my head. 'I don't think I'll be working on the boards again when I do get out,' I whispered, my throat feeling a bit hard and swollen. 'They tell me I'm disfigured for — for life.'

She clenched her hands on her knees. 'Forget it. You may be badly cut up, but there's ways and means. This plastic surgery racket can fix just about anything these days. You'll be okay in time, and right back in your old spot.'

She left soon afterwards, seeming to have something on her mind. I slept the rest of the day and night, and when I woke up the following morning I felt unbelievably better. Apart from the sore aching of my jaw and my burned eyelid, and the numb feeling in my toes, which were also in plaster casts, I was a lot more cheerful.

The doctor gave me a pleasant good morning when he came round, and I ventured to sound him about my disfigurement. 'How bad am I, Doctor? I'd like to know — the truth.'

'We can't say just yet,' he replied evasively.

'You must have an idea. Honestly, I'd feel better if you told me, rather than just lie here, wondering, being afraid, hoping and despairing.'

He nodded gravely. 'Very well. Your jaw and your broken toes will be all right in a short time. But you'll need false teeth — most of your own are gone — and you'll also be permanently scarred on the face, particularly the eyelid. We're afraid that, in healing, the tissues of the lid will draw together — that would mean your eyelid would be permanently screwed up.'

I tried to take it bravely, tried to laugh, and said: 'That'd mean I can't be the darling of the tired businessmen anymore, won't it?'

'Is that very important?' he said, smiling. 'Let the tired businessmen get along without you somehow.'

I was depressed all the rest of the day; was almost sorry I'd persuaded him to tell me the extent of my injuries. With only one sound eye, I didn't care to read. I just lay and thought, and my thoughts weren't very pleasant ones.

Maddie called in the afternoon again; there was a gleam in her eyes, and it didn't go even when I told her how bad I was with regard to the scars I had to expect. She said, when I had finished telling her: 'Don't you worry any more about it. There's a famous plastic surgeon who has a practice up on the coast, Palm Springs way. They reckon he can fix darned near anything, and that's where you're going.'

'But Maddie, how do you know he'll take my case?'

'Because I've already talked to him

long-distance, that's how. He's accepted already.'

'Oh, I can't do it, Maddie. He'll — he'll want a fortune to fix me up again. You know what these specialists are.'

'That's fixed too. From here on, every penny the Bexton makes goes towards putting you right.'

'No, I couldn't . . . '

'Nobody's *asking* you,' she growled. 'I'm *telling* you. Now just forget about it until it's time for you to leave this den of pain and suffering.'

I did as she asked, and didn't refer again to the matter. We talked about the show, and she told me about some new numbers she planned to fill my spot for the time being.

'Who's your star now?' I asked curiously.

She blushed a bit, looked at her toes, and said: 'Well, it may be a shock to you, but *I* am. They don't notice the wrinkles so much when I've plastered myself with make-up and got a blue spotlight playing on me. Besides, my legs are still in pretty good shape — look.' She raised her skirts

131

and grinned at me.

But I knew why she was taking my place. I didn't ask her, but it was plain enough — she was taking my place and my salary, and she was saving the money for me — just in case I didn't get well again. I found that out to be the truth, later.

Three long months dragged by while I stayed in that hospital. They didn't let me out until my jaw and toes were healed, and until I had the dressings off my features. When I finally did see my face in a mirror, I fainted.

I went home to the suite over the Bexton, with my face hidden by a veil; I felt I could never again take that veil off.

Before I left the hospital, the police came again for the umpteenth time; but as always, I simply told them I had no idea of who my assailants had been.

Maddie had staged a little party for me, with some of the girls from the show and one or two of the men. She hadn't thought about my scars — poor Maddie, she looked crestfallen when I sneaked into the bedroom without seeing them,

132

and told her she'd have to get them away. But she sent them off, and then she came back to me, and I took off my veil and showed her.

She tried her damnedest not to betray her revulsion. It wasn't really all that bad; but it was the eyelid — the twisted, screwed-up eyelid — that made it seem so horrible. I couldn't shut it; the membranes had been destroyed. I had to sleep with a patch over that eye. Finally Maddie managed to say: 'It isn't so bad, honey. It could be worse — and I'm dead sure this plastic surgeon can fix you up like new again. I've arranged for you to go to him next week.'

But at odd intervals during the night she kept looking at my face; her own face grew taut and grim the more she looked, and at length she stood up and said: 'I'm going along to the show now, kid. I don't suppose you want to come along too?'

'Not tonight, Maddie,' I told her. 'I couldn't face the curious stares I'd get.'

'I know how you feel. Well, don't get too down-hearted, honey. Read a book or something. I'll get back as soon as I can.'

I took her advice and read. When at last I glanced at the clock, it was twelve at night. I began to wonder what had happened to Maddie. She'd said she'd be right back, and she should have been in for eleven-thirty, that being so. I slipped on coat, hat and veil and went downstairs to the theatre proper. I found the place deserted; old Alec, the doorman, was just leaving for the night.

'Alec, have you seen Maddie?' I asked.

'Why yes, Miss Barry. She went out right after the curtain fell, and she'd got her street things on. No, I don't know where, miss.'

I went back upstairs and went to bed, for I was tired out. Maddie arrived back at about two o'clock, and I felt her climb in beside me. I didn't bother her with questions then, and when I rose in the morning she was still sleeping.

While I made coffee, I read the paper. It said:

'*GANGLAND SLAYING —*
MITZI LARUE
SHOT TO DEATH!'

134

12

Did Maddie Do It?

'In the early hours of this morning, Mitzi Larue, well-known woman racketeer whose night club and residence are at Harlem, was shot four times through the stomach, and died in considerable agony half an hour later.

'The police have learned that Miss Larue was, at the time of the attack, seated in her dining room, the windows of which open out onto an extensive lawn, and beyond that again, rows of tenement houses. The shots were apparently fired from the lawn, to which access could have been easily gained, and are from a small-calibre automatic.

'No clues have been found, and Superintendent Graddock says the case is extremely baffling. Miss

135

Larue's maid heard the shots and found her mistress writhing in pain on the floor, close to the open windows. The dead woman herself was unable to make any statement, as she almost immediately lost consciousness, recovering only minutes prior to her death; but it is assumed she was standing looking from the window, possibly attracted by some noise in the garden.

'A thorough search has failed to reveal any signs of the murderer.

'It is known that Miss Larue's activities were not such as made her a very popular citizen, and that many of her activities did indeed extend into the underworld of gangdom. Obviously the killing was perpetrated by a member or members of a rival gang with whom Miss Larue had had some misunderstanding.

'Investigations are proceeding.'

I had hardly finished reading when there were sounds of Maddie coming in from the bedroom. I hastily thrust the paper to one side as if I had not yet picked it up. Maddie looked tired and worn, and her eyes were sunken rather deeply into her head. She gave me a cheerful grin, though, and said: 'Say, you're up early. They must've taught you that in hospital, huh?'

'I've made coffee, Maddie,' I told her. 'And toast. Sit down and tuck in — then perhaps you ought to have a few more hours in bed — you look a little sick.'

She nodded tiredly. 'Sure I feel a little sick. Sorry I was late home last night, kiddo. Got myself mixed up in a sudden date. Unexpected, you know.'

'Oh — oh, yes, I know how it is. Don't worry.'

'And by the way . . . ' She broke off, turned, and looked me in the eyes. 'If anybody comes here asking where I was last night — not that they will, mind, but just in case — will you do me a big favour and tell them I was right here with you?'

I didn't know what to say for the minute. Then I went over to her, picked up the paper, and laid it down before her.

Her eyes shot across the headlines and down the column. Then she looked at me. 'I guess you've put two and two together and got the right answer, haven't you, Lucille?' I nodded. She sighed and said: 'Well, now what are you going to do about it?'

'Nothing, except back you up to the limit. Of course you stayed with me all last night. But I don't think they'll trace it to you, will they, Maddie?'

'No, kid, I think not. I pitched the rod right out into the river before I came back, and I took darned good care to leave no traces. They won't pin anything on me. They'll root around for some gang leader Maddie had a feud with — and they'll find plenty.'

'Why did you do it, Maddie? It was an awful risk to take.'

'Why? Hell, you think I was going to let her get away with what she did to you? No, honey, not likely. I gave it to her in the guts, so's it'd hurt like hell.' She sipped her coffee. 'Let's forget about it. Any more coffee?'

There was a sudden rap at the door,

and the theatre caretaker called: 'There's a guy down below wanting to see you ladies.'

Maddie's face tautened suddenly, and my own must have shown panic, for she said: 'Take it easy — it may be nothing.'

'Who — who is it?' I called. 'What does he want?'

'I don't know. Just said he wanted to see you, and that he was Superintendent Potter from Headquarters.'

Maddie shouted: 'Bring him up, Jake.' Then she whispered to me: 'Keep calm, kiddo. Wait and see what he wants. Maybe it's something about the show.'

Superintendent Potter was fat and fortyish. He looked exactly like a superintendent of police in every way. He came in and took a chair to which I invited him, then turned to me at once. 'Miss Barry,' he began, and my heart jumped, 'I've called to ask you again who beat you up that night. I feel sure you know more than you like to say. Cases of assault have been on the increase, and we must do something. If you can help in any way at all, we'd be grateful.'

'No, Superintendent. I'm really sorry, but I can't. I've told you that a dozen times in the last three months. If you put me under the third degree, I couldn't say another word about the matter.'

'Then how about someone who may have had a grudge against you?'

'I don't know of anyone.'

'You sure about that?' he asked, eyes boring into mine.

'Very sure.'

'Then how about Mitzi Larue?'

I didn't know what to say.

'We recently unearthed a young guy who calls himself a poet, who says you had an argument with the Larue woman the night you were beaten up. So?'

'Yes, it's true,' I agreed, biting my lip.

'Seems you two weren't over-fond of each other. So?'

'That's right too. Mitzi blamed me for taking her boyfriend from her and swore to get even.'

'Boyfriend?'

'Ricardo Corday.'

He tensed in his chair and sat upright stiffly. He fixed his two piercing eyes on me and rapped: 'I didn't know you were Corday's girlfriend. You know where he is now?'

'No. We quarreled and split up when he ran out of town. I have no idea where he could be right now.'

'So you took him from Mitzi, did you? Very interesting. And you had a quarrel with Mitzi Larue the night you were beaten up — just, in fact, before you were beaten up. Is that it? Yes? And *still* you say you didn't see who did it?'

'Yes, I still say that, Superintendent.'

He got up and walked to the door. 'Don't make much difference now, anyways. Maybe you didn't know Mitzi Larue was shot up at her home last night — or did you?'

Maddie simulated shock and gasped. 'Good God! *Mitzi* — *shot?* Why, we had no idea . . . '

'Nope? Then you must be pretty *blind*, sister. It's plastered all over the headlines of the paper you've stuck under your snoot.'

'Well, well,' said Maddie, 'so it is. But I only read the comic supplement, Super.

Can't get the hang of them three-syllable words.'

'And on top of that, I mustn't forget you're actresses,' he said thoughtfully. 'Good ones, I reckon — or maybe *not so good*. But you don't need to worry, girls; the department isn't going to press this case. Larue had too much pull in town for her own good. There's plenty of the top boys glad to see her go. I just thought I'd drop in and let you see we aren't so dumb as you may think. So long.'

We stared at each other for minutes when he had gone; then we both burst into a laugh and Maddie said: 'Could you tie that?'

'Next you know they'll be offering you a G-man's badge!' I told her, and we finished breakfast in an easier frame of mind.

★ ★ ★

Doctor Hatton Reginald Garner was delightful. He was tall, grey-eyed and blond-haired; he had even, white teeth and the nicest smile I'd ever seen. His skin was sun-bronzed and his arms and body lithe and supple. He looked far more like a professional sportsman than an eminent practitioner of plastic surgery.

His home was delightful, too. Set on the outskirts of Palm Springs, it was a big mellow mansion with carefully cultured lawns and wide, spacious flower gardens full of exotic blooms. It was a private home, not a sanatorium. I didn't know that until after I'd arrived. He greeted me politely and kindly, and didn't even seem to notice my veil. I was glad of that — I was sick of people peering at me as if I were some curiosity.

He had me shown to a beautiful room. Then, when I rejoined him downstairs, we took lunch on the patio facing a long, rolling stretch of countryside.

I put my foot in it at first by saying: 'Where are the other patients, Doctor?'

He raised his eyebrows at that and regarded me quizzically. 'Other patients, Miss Barry? There aren't any.'

'There aren't any? But — but isn't this a sanatorium?'

'It isn't even a nursing home.' He

143

smiled. 'Didn't your friend tell you about our arrangements?'

'Why no, I'm afraid she didn't.'

'Then I will. I ceased practising some years ago, when I inherited this estate from an uncle of mine. I now live an entirely useless life, you see. Your friend telephoned me and made me such in attractive offer to take your case, and pleaded so touchingly for me to do so, that I could hardly refuse. That's why you're here, Miss Barry — my solitary patient, to whom I can devote all my time — and I feel sure we'll get along well together.'

I murmured something mechanically. So that was what Maddie had done. I shuddered to think of how much this must have cost her and still would cost her. She probably hadn't told me the exact state of the arrangements because I'd have refused to go. Now it was too late.

He smiled at me. 'We needn't be too formal and ethical about all this, you see. While you're here, you must regard yourself as a guest and not a patient.

Now, if you'll step into my study we'll have a quick examination of these injuries of yours. I'm sure we'll be able to fix you up. I've been in touch with the doctor at the hospital, and he tells me they aren't as hopeless as they look.'

It wasn't embarrassing somehow to show my scars to him. He was neither repulsed nor obviously sympathetic. He simply said: 'The face won't present any difficulties. How about the stomach?'

That was embarrassing, even before him; but he inspected me in a cold professional way, and when I blushed, he smiled and said: 'Try and regard me as one of those tired businessmen you used to entertain.'

His examination finished, I said uncertainly: 'Can you — can you do anything for me, Doctor?'

'Certainly I can. I should say another six to eight months will see you almost as good as new. I even predict a return to the stage for you.' Then his tone became serious, and he took me by the shoulders. 'It will hurt, Miss Barry,' he said gravely. 'It will hurt like — well, to put it unprofessionally, like *hell*. But you must have faith in me, trust me. That way I can accomplish wonders.'

'I will, Doctor. I can stand the pain if only I don't look so hideous when it's all over.'

He gripped my hand. 'You don't look hideous — the scars don't count. In my eyes they don't exist, except as a problem to be erased. I look at you and they vanish. I see you only as you were — and, by God, as you will be again, if modern surgery can fix you up. And it can.'

He didn't discuss the subject again that day. We had a pleasant dinner, and towards ten o'clock he said: 'Off to bed with you. You may have been used to late hours in New York, but you have to do as the doctor orders here, you know. And in case you're worried about the proprieties, here's the key of your room. Mrs. Craig, my housekeeper, sleeps just along the passage from you, so you'll be quite safe.'

'I know I will, Doctor. Thanks for everything.'

He escorted me to the top of the stairs. 'Have a good night's rest. I generally get up at eight and take a turn on the horses — I have stables about a mile from here. If you feel you'd like to join me tomorrow, come down when you hear the first gong. And by the way, since we aren't being ethical on this case, have you any objections to my calling you Lucille?'

'None at all, Doctor. Provided I can call you Reggie.'

'Delighted.' He grinned and watched me all the way to my room.

Inside I stood with the key in my hand for a minute. I looked at the lock, then at the photograph of the doctor over the fireplace. Then I slipped the key onto the table without locking the door. I'd never felt so safe in my life before. And the doctor — Reggie!

Already I was looking forward to this long stay at his wonderful home. Already I felt unreasonably attracted to him — perhaps because he was almost the first decent man I'd met in my hitherto sordid life. I fell asleep, still thinking about him . . .

13

Interlude for Love

I'm not going to say a whole lot about the six months that followed. Most of the time I was in bed, and a lot of it was in considerable, wearisome pain. Grafting is one hell of a thing to have to undergo — I can't attempt to describe the way it wears you down and down until you're sick and tired and wondering if it's all worthwhile.

But Reggie — whom I knew as a fine, decent man — helped me through the worst of it. He was always there when I wanted him; and from being more or less professional in his regard of me, now he seemed to want to fix me up properly from a more personal angle. I grew to love him during those months, and the times when we went riding brought back the early days of my life to me, making me feel nostalgic about the

148

countryside and open-air life.

He was surprised to find I was a good horse rider. He'd thought I wouldn't know how, but when I told him I'd been raised on a farm, he understood. Riding's one of those things you never forget, once learned — like bicycling, skating, or swimming. I was out of practice but I soon put that right.

In the evenings we used to talk about anything and everything. He told me all about himself — how his parents were wealthy Maine people; how he'd had life made easy for him. But I didn't think it was so easy to train for surgery — I couldn't have done it.

In return I had to tell him my story — and I really wanted to. There was something about him that inspired confidence. Call it his bedside manner if you like, but it was something more than that. I felt in tune with him all the time, and knew he wouldn't blame me but would sympathise — and I needed his sympathy. I told him the whole tale, not even omitting mention of the dirty deal Riccy gave me. The only thing I didn't tell him was who killed Mitzi; but I expect, from the rest of the story, he guessed. He said he'd like to meet Maddie; said she must be a fine person.

He and the nurse he had, between them, took wonderful care of me. Then came the day when my dressings were due to come off. There was a strained look on his face as he sat me on a chair in the study. I knew he was praying everything was as it should be — that the healing was complete and that I was perfect again. The scars on my stomach had already gone — were, at least, hardly noticeable.

He unwrapped my face, and as the bandages came off a slow smile broke across his features. I didn't dare speak — I myself hadn't seen myself in a mirror for a long time, and had no idea how I was progressing.

He stood looking at me for a long time; then he picked up a hand mirror and gave it to me . . .

It was wonderful! I could hardly tell I'd had any scars at all, and my damaged eyelid was quite perfect again. I was the same Lucille Barry that I had been before!

Impulsively I threw my arms around his neck and kissed him. He took it smilingly, but didn't attempt to return the embrace — and I thought that rather funny, for unless my intuition was wrong I could have sworn he was in love with me.

He detached himself, held me at arm's length, and said: 'I'm glad you're all right again, Lucille. Maddie is coming up to take you back to town tomorrow. There's nothing more for me to do, and I wrote her yesterday.'

I nodded. Suddenly, at the thought of leaving him, all the joy had gone out of me. I hadn't considered what my recovery would mean, but now it came home to me. I was cured — I was whole again. There wouldn't even be a chance to see him again; no excuse to call on him. And he still seemed to regard me more as a friend than — well, than anything else. Perhaps I was wrong about him being in love with me. Maybe, cut off as he was from women up here, anyone would have stirred his interest.

Then the prospect of seeing Maddie again brightened me up. I hadn't seen her for two months; he'd asked her not to come during the latter end of the treatment because I got too excited about the show and the theatre and everything. Besides which, there was always the pleasure of returning to the theatre, which I loved so much, pretty soon. And he might still speak before I left; give me some hint, some sign.

We spent a quiet night talking, as usual, and Reggie remained warm but not affectionate. I know that at the least hint I'd have thrown myself into his arms, through the love I felt for him. He had been the one decent man in my life whom I knew really well, and I was frightened — yes, frightened — of him going out of it forever. But he gave no sign; and when I went to bed, rather late, I was too tired to think much about it. I decided to take it as well as I could, and if he didn't want me I was determined not to lower myself by throwing my love at him and having it politely and regretfully thrown back in my face.

The morning was chilly, but there was a cheerful sun shining down. It was an ideal day for travelling, but my pleasure was still damped by the thought of leaving Reggie. The nearer the time drew, the more distant he seemed to grow, until at last, he cornered me in the flower garden and said: 'Well, I'm off to meet the ten-fifteen now. I'll bring Maddie back in the car. You'll be all right here, won't you?'

'Why, yes — why shouldn't I be? Nurse is helping me to pack.'

He nodded, then stood looking at a rose bush. He suddenly plucked one, pushed it through the buttonhole of my costume coat, and said: 'You go well together — you and roses.'

It was an awkward speech, made too awkwardly for me to respond as I so longed to. I said: 'Flatterer.'

He grinned, a bit feebly I thought, and said: 'I think we'd better say goodbye now, then we won't have it all to go through in front of Maddie. Knowing how she can talk, I doubt we'd have the chance then.'

I felt close to tears. 'Doctor — Reggie — I can't ever thank you enough. You've been wonderful.'

He smiled. 'Forget it. I enjoyed having you around.'

'Will you — will you miss me?'

'Well, that's only natural, isn't it? I suppose in time I'll get used to the idea that you aren't here anymore.'

That put the damper on me entirely. I said stiffly: 'Has Maddie paid all we owe? The fees?'

'Yes; that's all taken care of.'

I held out my hand and he took it. Then, unable to resist, I leaned forward and kissed him lightly. He said: 'Thanks. I'll push off to the station now and pick up Maddie.'

He went, and as the car roared towards the town I started to cry there in the garden. I wiped my eyes and went in to pack.

When he got back with Maddie, I was all ready to go. Maddie was bubbling over with excitement, said there was a grand reception waiting at the theatre, and asked Reggie if he'd come back with us and take his share of the honour for having fixed me up so wonderfully. He shook his head, apologised, and said he didn't think he could leave the estate at the moment.

We had lunch, then he drove us back to the two-thirty for New York. I was feeling worse and worse about it all, the closer we got to the station. The prospect of the long train journey was incredibly depressing — how different it would have seemed if he had only agreed to go back with us and stay a while. But he himself didn't betray any signs of despondency. He chatted cheerfully of this and that, pointing out spots of local interest, and laughing with Maddie as he showed her the bump of ground where I had fallen from my horse the first day out.

Then we were at the station, with half an hour to wait for the train. Reggie suddenly became silent, and after a few minutes on the platform he said: 'Do you mind if I leave now? I have some rather important engagements to keep, and I'd like to be in time for them.'

'Not at all,' I said. 'Please don't wait

— we'll be all right!'

He took my hand again and pressed it. 'It's been nice having you; and if ever you need any similar treatment — God forbid — but if you ever do, you know who to come to. And it's been nice knowing you, too, Maddie. Take good care of her.'

'Don't worry.' Maddie grinned.

He gave my hand a last final clasp, then turned and walked out of the station. At the barrier he turned again and waved; then he was gone — and two small tears rolled down my cheeks.

I noticed Maddie staring at me curiously. She said suddenly: 'You love him, don't you?'

I nodded miserably. She went on: 'Then why are you beating it, you silly kid?'

'What else can I do? He doesn't care for me.'

'Doesn't he? Then why did he refuse to take money from me for your treatment?'

'He — he did that?'

'He did. Wouldn't take a cent.'

'But — Maddie — why didn't you tell me? Why didn't you explain that?'

She grinned. 'It isn't too late, kid. Dash after him now.'

'Oh, I couldn't do that — he'd think — '

'He wouldn't think anything. Go on, you dopey cluck.'

I shook my head stubbornly. After all, perhaps he had just refused the fees because he liked my company. Perhaps. 'I couldn't go after him, Maddie, I couldn't. Why didn't he speak if he was fond of me?'

'Why? Because he isn't the type of guy to speak, that's why. I thought you could see that for yourself. You were under his roof and under his protection — he didn't have the right to make love to you, and you know it. If he had, something might have happened, and he's the kind of guy who wouldn't ever have forgiven himself for that. Besides, he probably didn't have any idea how you felt about him — didn't want to embarrass you by letting you see he was fond of you. Now get after him, for God's sake.'

I was still stubborn; I stood there, tears in my eyes, shaking my head. I just couldn't do it.

Maddie delivered a fancy curse word, then started running for the barrier herself. She rushed through and out of the depot. I heard the roar of a car, then her voice shouting: 'Hey! *Hey! Come back here, you dope!* She's nuts about you!'

I went a bright crimson colour and stood, hoping he hadn't heard her; hoping that if he had, he'd ignore her. I felt terrible. People were staring at me and grinning. And then Maddie came through the barrier again — and Reggie was with her!

He came to a halt about three feet from me, and there was a new look on his face, a look he hadn't ever worn before. I stood there, red and flustered, uncertain what to do. Maddie said: 'Well, you pair of mutts — what're you waiting for?'

'Lucille . . . ' he began, just as I said: 'Reggie . . . ' Our remarks clashed, and we both stopped and grinned feebly.

'Go ahead,' he said generously.

'You were saying . . . ?' I asked him.

Maddie said: 'Did you ever see anything like it? What're you putting on a cross-talk act for? Why don't you get some *action* into it? For God's sake . . . '

She gave me a push that sent me straight for him; when I got there his arms were waiting, ready to receive me. He looked at Maddie and winked, then he looked at me and said: 'I didn't know, Lucille — I thought you didn't care about me. Well, not in *that* way.'

'And I thought the same, Reggie,' I murmured happily. 'I had no idea you could care anything about — about a burlesque dancer.'

He laughed at that. 'It wouldn't matter if you were a Japanese Geisha girl — what you are hasn't anything to do with it. Or how you look. I loved you, I think, from the first week you got here.'

'I loved you before that,' I whispered. 'I think I must've dreamed often about you.'

He smiled again, and then he brought his lips down to mine . . .

I was wildly happy; I didn't care about the crowd of curious rubbernecks who were grinning at us. I could hear Maddie saying: 'All right folks, pass along. Ain't you never seen a couple in love before?

Give 'em air, give 'em air!'

The train came rocketing down the tracks and screamed to a halt in the station. Maddie said: 'Well, here's my train. I'll leave you two to it. So long, Lucille — so long, Reginald, my lad.'

'Hold on,' he told her, releasing me. 'You don't think I'd let Lucille miss that swell reception you had set for her, do you? She's going with you.'

'No dice.' Maddie grinned. 'I ain't blind — she'd be bored to tears. She wants to stay with you.'

'She *will*,' he said, pulling me towards the train. 'I'm coming too, just like this.'

'But your car . . . ' I stammered.

He laughed. 'I can phone a garage later.'

14

The Bexton Again

The theatre hadn't changed much in the months I'd been away, except that my name had gone from the posters, and now Maddie's was in its place. But there was the same company, and they all showed how glad they were to see me back again. We had quite a rousing party in the suite above the theatre, and later Reggie and I went out front to see the show.

It was afterwards, before he left for the hotel he'd booked rooms at, and before Maddie had gotten back to the suite, that he got really serious about things. He said: 'Of course, Lucille, you'll marry me, won't you?'

I smiled at him. 'Try and stop me, Reggie.'

'And — you'll give up the stage?'

'Of course, dear. We'll live at your estate.'

'Fine.' He grinned. 'I couldn't have you working, of course, and I know how attached you are to all this. Do you really think you could give it up for me?'

'A hundred times over, Reggie; and then, I can always come down on odd visits — you won't mind that, will you?'

He said he wouldn't, and he let that side of it rest there. He went on: 'When — I mean, how soon shall we get married, then?'

'That's up to you,' I told him. 'Far as I'm concerned, it can be as soon as you wish after we've settled details.'

'How about your parents?'

I suddenly remembered them; how strict they'd been with me. But after all, they were my parents. They had a right to know I was planning to get married. 'I'd like to call on them, Reggie, and tell them. I haven't seen them since I ran away.'

'Think they'll approve of me?' He smiled.

'I know it. But your parents — will they approve of me?'

He slipped an arm around my waist, kissed me, and said: 'Don't you worry about that. They'll love you, I know.'

'You say they live in Maine?'

'That's right. I thought we'd drive there sometime and see them, before we tie the knot. That okay?'

'Yes, it's fine. We can kill two birds with one stone that way. My parents live quite near Maine, and we could easily call on them before we go on to your folks' home.'

We settled it that way; Reggie planned to stay until the end of the week, then he was going to return and bring down his car for me, so that we could take it easy driving to Maine. It was a very pleasant week, buying in clothes for the trip; I was out of touch with the latest fashions, and needed an entirely new wardrobe.

Reggie came with me, carrying parcels uncomplainingly. Maddie, at my request, had kept the news of my return to New York dark from the press. I hadn't felt like being swarmed on by nosey reporters and cameramen; but one afternoon, towards the end of Reggie's visit, I was caught nicely down town outside the *Sentinel* office. Two staff photographers came out, and as they looked at me I saw them nudging each other. Then they came over holding their cameras as if they meant action.

One said to me: 'Miss Cutie Dubarry, aren't you, lady?'

I glanced at Reggie and saw he was frowning a little. Hastily I said: 'You're mistaken. My name's Jones.'

He winked at his pal. 'Funny. We did hear Miss Dubarry was back in town — without any disfigurement. You *are* Dubarry, aren't you? Come on, give us a break.'

I was about to deny it again, when Maddie came from the shop she'd been in and joined us. That settled it for them — they knew Maddie, and seeing her with me they didn't need to know any more. Their cameras were clicking in no time, taking photos of Maddie, Reggie and myself standing there.

'Please — I don't want any publicity. I'm out of the burlesque show for good.'

'How about a pic of you showing those swell legs of yours, Miss Dubarry?'

Reggie growled in his throat. 'Why

don't you two vultures beat it, while you're still able? The lady doesn't want to be bothered.'

'Yeah? An' who are you to know what the lady wants and doesn't want, buddy?'

'Only the man who's going to marry her,' Reggie grunted.

'What? Why, that's swell! How about one of you kissin' her, mister? Give us a break, c'mon? Dubarry getting hitched! Say, this rates headlines! What a story — and with pictures.'

'What's your name, mister?' asked the second photographer.

'Don't give him that, Reggie,' I said quickly.

'Okay, we'll find out,' said the newspaper man with a grin. 'It's been swell seeing you and getting this story — it'll be an exclusive to the *Sentinel*, won't it? Or do you intend to give any more interviews to anyone else?'

'No. I'd rather you didn't use that story, too.'

'Sorry, miss. We have to live, don't we? I've personally got five hungry kids to support, an' this'll help make it six. I ought to get a raise for this.'

'Me too,' said the second. 'Thanks, Miss D. So long.'

Like a couple of scavengers who'd just made a good meal of a corpse, they scooted into the *Sentinel* buildings. The three of us stared at one another.

'Well,' said Maddie, 'that cooks it. By tomorrow we'll be snowed under with news-noses trying to grab off exclusive interviews with leg pictures. Can you beat that?'

Reggie said: 'Good job I won't be here — I'd lose my temper with them, I'm afraid. I'll leave tonight for Palm Springs and get back as quick as I can with the car, then we'll skip town and throw them off the scent.'

He'd gone by the time the deluge broke; the evening *Sentinel* carried the story in big headlines:

'DUBARRY COMES TO TOWN!
RESUSCITATED BURLESQUE
BEAUTY HITS NEW YORK AGAIN'

By our special correspondents.

166

'Dee-lightful, dee-licious, dee-lovely Dubarry — better known to our readers perhaps as *Cutie Dubarry of the Bexton Burlesque* — was today interviewed exclusively by the Sentinel. She told our reporters that she means to give up burlesque and concentrate on raising a family; for handsome ex-plastic surgeon Hatton Reginald Garner, who accompanied Miss Dubarry and who told our reporters he is engaged to her.

'Miss Dubarry looks as lovely — if not lovelier — than ever, and of the scars she sustained during a gang beat-up recently there is no trace. Readers will remember that it was rumoured at that time that the attack might have been instigated by racketeer Ricardo Corday, who skipped town with the feds hot on his tail and is still missing. Miss Dubarry and Corday had been a twosome for some time, and it was believed a quarrel took place between them when the net closed in on Corday.

'We regret that Miss Dubarry was

firm about not giving our photographers any pictures of her gorgeous legs, but we have raided the files for the ones we reproduce below.

'The other photographs were taken this afternoon, and by comparison it will be seen that Miss Dubarry's looks have not suffered in the least through her unfortunate experience.'

★ ★ ★

I felt worried about Reggie — I wouldn't have minded much if they hadn't gotten his name, but they had. It wasn't nice for a man to be plastered all over the front a news-sheet with a dame as notorious as myself. All that stuff about Riccy, and those photos they'd dug up, showing me wearing nothing but a G-string, a thin brassiere and a pleasant smile!

Maddie was fine the way she kept off the reporters. At about nine o'clock they stopped coming. I was glad, for ever since Maddie had gone down to the show I hadn't dared answer any rings at the bell.

It was stuffy upstairs, and I put on a

cape and went down for a breath of air. I'd hardly got outside the door when a young man with a battered trilby grabbed my arm. 'You're Dubarry, aren't you?'

'I — '

'You are? Swell. Let's get inside.'

'Hold on,' I said sharply. 'I don't know you!'

'The name's Larsen.'

'But I haven't met you before.'

'I haven't met you, so that makes us square. Let's go up to your rooms.'

'But — what do you want?'

He looked mysterious, put a finger to his lips, glared all around as if expecting the walls to sprout ears, and whispered: 'Got a word for you from Riccy.'

'Riccy? Ricardo Corday?'

'The same white-haired boy.'

'Then I don't want to hear it. Please leave me alone.'

'You'll be sorry,' he told me, and suddenly I thought I'd better find out all I could about Riccy. He was such a cagey guy that I felt he might get up to any tricks — especially if he'd read about my engagement.

I opened the door, which was right next to the stage entrance. He followed me in quickly and came up the stairs. I nodded him to a chair, took one myself, and said: 'Well?'

'Nice place you got here,' he said appreciatively, looking about him. 'Very nice. Now about this offer . . . '

'Offer? What offer?'

'This offer my paper is willing to make you for a few pics of your stomach . . . '

My head was whirling. I stammered: 'Paper? *Paper?* But — how about Riccy? The message?'

'Oh, that was a gag to get in. I've been turned away all day, but I didn't mean to be turned away tonight. My rag's willing to pay you five thousand bucks for exclusive pics of your, er, your stomach. You know, where you got badly cut.'

I got to my feet, my face a fiery red. I snapped: 'I think the suggestion's disgusting, Mr. Larsen. Be good enough to leave before I call the police and have you thrown out.'

'But five grand, doesn't that tempt you?'

'It tempts me to kick you out myself.'

'Okay, don't get sore. You didn't used to mind showing *more* than your stomach to the public — and five grand's a fair offer.'

'I think you're the most boorish man I ever met,' I snapped, and held open the door.

'Shut the door, kid, it's drafty. And I haven't finished spouting to you yet.'

'You may think not, but you have. Are you going?'

'Nope.'

I shrugged my shoulders and crossed to the telephone. I dialed the stage entrance, got the doorman on the line, and said: 'Have you got a couple of stagehands to spare? There's a nosey reporter up here who wants throwing out.'

'Sure, Miss Barry, I'll send up a couple of the boys right away.'

I downed the phone again and glared at the reporter, who was sitting back, grinning. He said: 'Don't try that fake phone call stuff on me.'

'You think it was a fake?' I asked.

'Sure, I know you dames. Actually

you're looking for all the publicity you can grab and then some. But you think if you pull a mysterious line it'll make the boys play the story up more, don't you? Well, you don't need to do that with me. We'll play you up. I got the editor's permission to offer you two grand for your story of how you and this Garner guy got together. How about that if the other offer doesn't tempt you?'

'I don't know who you work for, Mr. Larsen, but you and your editor both should be prevented from annoying innocent people like this. Now you'd better get out before the boys arrive.'

He dangled a leg across the couch. 'How long're you going to keep up this mystery-woman stunt? You used to be hot enough on publicity when you were Queen of the Bexton. You aren't going to tell me that's right about you giving that up, are you?'

'I'm not going to tell you anything, as a matter of fact.'

He sighed, lit a cigarette, and said: 'I can wait . . .'

There was a rap at the door. I opened it

and said: 'Come in, boys.'

Two of the big, tough-looking scene shifters came in and looked around. One of them said: 'So where's this nosey newshound you want disemboweled, miss?'

I pointed to Larsen, who'd dropped his smoke and was gaping at them. He gasped. 'Say, was that on the level about having me slung out?'

'What do you think?'

'If you expect the papers to give you a good break when you treat their representatives this way, you're nuts.'

'I don't want the papers to give me any breaks. I just want to be left alone.'

He got up and said: 'I'll go — don't get upset, boys.'

'You're too late,' I told him. 'You *asked* for it. Better throw him out, boys, and then maybe he won't be in such a hurry to get back!' They grabbed him roughly and jerked him out. The sound of strife died away down the stairs . . .

15

This Burlesque Woman!

Reggie got back with the car the following Friday. During the days that had elapsed, I had left the suite at the Bexton, because of the incessant nuisance reporters constituted, and had taken rooms at an obscure hotel on the edge of the town. Here I was comparatively free from hindrance, and I continued my shopping expedition in the less fashionable portion of the town.

Maddie sent Reggie right around when he got back; and I showed him the newspaper cutting, wondering how he'd take it. He didn't take it too well; his brow knitted into a frown, and he muttered a curse or two under his breath.

'I'm sorry, Reggie,' I apologised. 'Perhaps we should call it all off . . .'

'No, no, Lucille. It isn't your fault. I knew all this when I asked you to marry me; and as I said before, I don't care what happened in the past. It's just that I've been thinking about my people — they're Maine society, and on the whole I think it would be as well not to mention anything of your past to them. We'll say you're a — well, a secretary in the city. That'll do — they don't have to know everything.'

'I see. If they did they might disapprove, is that it?'

'Naturally. But Lucille, you aren't going to be funny about that fact, are you? If you had a son, and he planned to marry a woman who'd been . . . well, from your point of view, notorious, would you approve? Frankly?'

'No,' I sighed. 'No, I wouldn't. All right, Reggie. I won't be melodramatic about it. Let's tell them I'm a secretary.'

'How about the papers? Do they reach Maine, I wonder?'

'Not a chance. The *Sentinel*'s a New York local. Copies aren't sent further than a fifty-mile radius.'

We said goodbye for the time being, to Maddie the day after, and began driving down, staying at hotels on the way. It was an enjoyable trip, and even now that we were engaged, Reggie was still a perfect gentleman, never expecting anything more than a conventional good-night kiss or the opportunity to put his arm round my waist. I felt I could be truly happy with him, and looked forward to our being really married, so that we could know each other as people in love must know each other.

The plan was to call first on my folks, whom I was now looking forward to seeing again, then continue to Reggie's parents' home and stay over there a few days. Early in the morning we reached the farmstead where I'd been raised. Down in the west meadow I could see my father taking the cows to pasture; from the chimney of the farmhouse came a column of smoke, showing me that Mother was still an early riser.

I left Reggie in the car until I'd made my reunion with my folks. I crept along to the door, pushed it gently open, and tiptoed into the kitchen.

Mother was at the fireplace, boiling a large kettle of water; she didn't hear me come in, didn't know I was there until I crept across and kissed her lightly on the back of her greying hair. Then she swung around with an exclamation, stared long and hard at me as if she could hardly recognise me, and suddenly threw her arms around my neck and pressed her worn cheek against me.

She was crying softly; and for the first time I realised, no matter how strict she had been, just how much my running away must have broken her heart. I soothed her and took her to a chair, then sat her down in it. I thought it best to give her the same story as I'd decided to give to Reggie's folks. I explained I'd had no luck as a journalist, but was doing nicely as secretary. Then I called Reggie in and introduced him as my prospective fiancé, and she seemed duly impressed.

'Ye should not have run away, Alice,' she said, and it brought all my childhood back to hear her using the name I had discarded and almost forgotten in the years that had passed. 'But I'm right glad to know ye're doing so well. I'll have to call your father — he'll be right pleased to see ye again.' She went out and I could hear her calling across the fields: 'Harry! Harry — Alice is back.'

I didn't know how he'd take it; I certainly thought he'd be glad to know I was all right, but I expected a lot of recriminations from him for running off as I had. But never in my whole life did I feel as embarrassed as I did when he walked in and stood just inside the doorway staring. For the first words out of his mouth were: '*Get out of here!*'

I stood staring at him with my mouth wide open. Reggie gave an unbelieving gasp. My mother exclaimed: 'Harry! What are ye saying to the girl?'

He walked further in, came across and confronted me. His hard suntanned features were like a mahogany carving; his lips set grimly across his drawn cheeks; his eyes bitter, burning orbs that pierced right through my outer finery and seemed to see all the sordidness I'd concealed underneath.

'I said *get out*. Neither your mother nor I want to have a thing to do with ye. Get.'

178

My mother hurried over and shoved herself between us. Her face was tear-stained, not tears of joy now, but tears of hurt surprise. 'Don't talk that way to her, Harry. She's our own flesh and blood, you can't send her away. Ye're making her look silly in front of the young man that's set to marry her.'

'Then he's a bigger fool than he looks,' growled my father surlily. 'Or mebbe he don't know.'

'What've you got agen her?' demanded my mother. 'Mebbe she run off, and that wasn't right, but she's doing well for herself in the city as a secretary — we can't blame her, Harry.'

He laid his hands on her shoulders and muttered: 'I didn't want nor intend to tell ye this, Meg — I didn't think she'd have the crust to show her face in this house agen — but now I don't intend to let ye be deceived by her. Here — I was sent this cutting by one of the neighbours . . . '

He opened his wallet and threw the paper cutting on the table. I knew what it was before I even saw it. The *Sentinel* article! I waited, tears almost flowing, while my mother read it. Finally she looked up wearily, unable to say anything.

My father went on: 'I don't want her in my house. She can go and get back to them fancy friends of hers, showing off her body and carrying on with hoodlums. We don't want her like hanging around a decent household.'

My mother said sadly: 'Is this here picture one of you, Alice?'

I hung my head in shame. Suddenly the enormity of what I'd done, of how I'd made my living, came home to me. Here, with folks as decent as my own were, it seemed magnified out of all proportion. I nodded; Reggie was silent.

'Then I think ye'd better go, girl,' she said, her voice now as hard as my father's. 'Ye're father's right — we don't want ye.'

Reggie stepped forward; he was awkward and uncomfortable, but he didn't like to see me treated like that. He began: 'Don't adopt this attitude to her, please. You don't understand the position she was in — I've heard the whole tale and I'm willing to *marry* her.'

'I understand one thing,' snapped my

father. 'She was old enough to know wrong from right, and what she did ain't right by no means. She's disgraced the mother that bore her, and she isn't wanted. And as for you, young feller, you'd be sensible to forget your idea about marrying her. Now I'd like ye to leave — ye're upsetting her mother and meself.'

Reggie didn't try to reason anymore; he put his arm round me tenderly and led me out. I thought I'd got pretty hard during the years I'd been in burlesque, but now I found I wasn't that tough that the scene I've described didn't cut through and through me.

'They're right,' I whispered to Reggie as we got in the car.

'No — they just don't want to understand.'

'No, they're right,' I said, hurting myself, but determined to get it cleared out in my own mind. 'There wasn't any excuse for what I did. How could there be?'

'Don't torment yourself. It's the atmosphere of this place where you were

181

brought up that's troubling you. Once we've left it behind you'll find your views are broadening again. You can't say a woman's bad because she chooses to make her living from her beauty. Good God! Why, my own sister was an artist's model before Father made his pile.'

'That isn't the same — that's art. Burlesque is . . . different. I didn't see it that way before.'

'But it isn't. Look at people like Maddie — real people! You can't condemn a person with a heart that big just because she picks an easy way. And if your own conscience is square, what else matters?'

'It was, but it isn't now. They've made me realise how wrong I've been. Nothing you say can alter that, Reggie. I feel as low as the lowest woman in the Bowery. Queen of Burlesque? Queen of Loose Living would be nearer the mark. I hate myself.'

'That's ridiculous. Whatever you did with your physical side, you stayed decent in your mind. I know that, Lucille. And that's the part of you I'm marrying —

that's what counts. Besides, those days are all over from now on. You don't need to worry ever again about things like that.'

By the time we reached Maine itself, I felt a bit better. I still couldn't forget my parents' scorn and disappointment in the way I'd chosen to go; but I hoped, with Reggie's help, that I'd be able to live down the past. Now I was keener than ever on working the secretary story on his parents. I hoped to God they hadn't also had a copy of the *Sentinel*. If they had, I knew I should die on the spot.

They were waiting for us to arrive; Reggie had wired them to say we were coming down, and rooms had been prepared. He introduced me first of all to a tall, thin white-haired lady in a fashionable gown. This was his mother. There was no warmth in her greeting; her hand took mine and held it limply. Her own hand was like a dry, thin stick. She said: 'How do you do, Miss Barry. I hope you had a pleasant journey?'

'Thank you, it was very enjoyable, Mrs. Garner.'

'So this is the girl you're going to

marry, my boy?' said his father, and I liked him at once. He was round and tubby and kindly-looking, a shocking contrast to the dry stick of a woman he had chosen to spend his life with. He gripped my hand, then drew me down towards him and kissed my cheek. 'Lovely, my boy, lovely. I never thought you'd get such a beautiful woman to marry a sober judge of a feller like you. How did you do it?'

'I knew you'd like her, Dad,' said Reggie boyishly, for all his thirty-eight years. 'Landing her wasn't so hard — you see, this is the girl I wrote and told you had had an accident, and whom I was treating at my estate in Palm Springs.'

'Reggie,' said his mother suddenly, 'you — you don't mean you — *have* to get married, do you?'

He flushed to the roots of his hair, and I felt as if she'd slapped me a blow in the face. He said: 'What's wrong with you, Mother? Of course I don't mean anything like that. Lucille will wonder what on earth kind of family I've got if you say things of that sort.'

'I'm sorry; I wasn't thinking. Please forgive me, Miss Barry.'

We went in to lunch at once, but I knew I had an enemy in his mother. I knew perfectly well that she'd said that purposely to make me feel uncomfortable to show me she didn't put that kind of thing past me.

Lunch was a silent affair; once or twice Reggie's father tried to speak, but a glance from his wife quelled him. Reggie seemed to be still upset from that opening remark of his mother's, and I myself was feeling too low altogether to talk, after the nasty things I'd had hurled at me that day.

Lunch over, I was shown to a room that was to be mine. It was far up, near the servants' quarters, and was small and poky and ill-furnished. I wondered if Reggie knew what his mother had prepared for me, and what he would say if he found out. However I said nothing, and when he announced his intention of driving into town to see one or two of his old friends, I could see he didn't want me to go along with him. A man doesn't at these times.

I watched him drive away, then went into the massive library. I thumbed through one or two books, feeling sad and fed up with everything. I was gazing out of the window when the door opened and Mrs. Garner walked in. Behind her, looking ill at ease, came her tubby husband. She came straight to the point without any tact or delicacy.

'Miss Barry, we would like to have a word with you.'

'Of course, Mrs. Garner.'

'It's about our son, Reginald. We'd like to know if you are quite serious with regard to accepting his offer of marriage?'

'Naturally I am,' I told her. 'Why should you think that I'm not?'

She paused; evidently what she was going to say next wasn't easy to put, even for a woman like her. Then she shrugged and said: 'I understand most women of your type merely get engaged to a man so that you can either sue him for breach of promise or be bought off. If you do marry him, it will only be for his money.'

'Mrs. Garner,' I said steadily, 'please

explain what you mean by women of my type? I don't understand you.'

'Surely it should be obvious. I refer to burlesque women and all actresses in general — oh, yes, Miss Barry, we've seen the *Sentinel*.'

16

How Much Will You Take?

I didn't speak after that. I couldn't. I could only wonder hopelessly just who *hadn't* seen that *Sentinel* article.

She went on: 'One of my friends in New York sent me a copy. She thought I ought to know what was going on.'

'Why?' I demanded. 'Reggie is thirty-eight, isn't he? He knows his own mind.'

'Not necessarily.' She smiled coldly. 'Even a man of thirty-eight can be momentarily fascinated by — a person like yourself. Indeed, even a much older man . . . ' and she shot a scathing and significant glance at her tubby husband, who wilted visibly.

So her friends had thought she ought to know what was going on, had they? How I hated those nosey interfering people — they weren't friends, I was sure of that. They did things like sending that cutting out of sheer maliciousness — it had been similar 'well-meaning' neighbours who had acquainted my father with the life I had found for myself. I was beyond feeling ashamed now; all I felt was a hot, burning anger that the things I'd discarded forever should rise up to be the cause of my persecution now. Why didn't people leave me alone? Why had they to hound me down and sneer and scoff at me, and think me not a decent associate for ordinary people, just because I'd been in burlesque?

And as I turned on her to tell her what I thought, I realised it would always be that way! People like Mrs. Garner and my father would always look down on me, scorn me, for the way I'd chosen to make my living. It was only with real people, people without any hypocrisy about them, that I'd find any understanding — folks like Maddie, and Reggie, and the little world of burlesque that was my real home; people whose morals might not have satisfied the tastes of a parson, but whose hearts were as big as they could possibly be without bursting altogether.

So I didn't jump at her as I'd meant to. Instead I said: 'Have you anything more to say?'

'Much more, Miss Barry — or would you feel more at home if I called you Dubarry?'

'It doesn't matter. Go on.'

'You must give Reggie up. I won't see him thrown away on a — a person — like yourself.'

'You think he's too good for me? Surely that view's a little old-fashioned in the nineteen twenties, Mrs. Garner? I seem to have read this exact plot in some Mid-Victorian novel — one of those with yellow covers, which shocked its generation. You would fit one of the less likeable characters to the life.'

'Really!' she said, her eyebrows lifting. 'How dare *you* insult *me*?'

'How dare *you* insult *me*?' I asked in return.

Reggie's father stepped forward here. He said: 'Look here, dear, why not stand aside and not try to interfere with the young people? If they love each other, I daresay — '

'Kindly keep out of this,' snapped his wife drily. 'I mean to save Reggie from this — this burlesque woman — if I possibly can do so. Miss Barry, how much will you take?'

'Take?'

'To give up Reggie.'

My first impulse was to snap an angry reply back at her. But on second thought I refrained from giving way. I decided to play with her for a while, as she deserved, and said thoughtfully: 'I see. You want to buy me off? Well, Mrs. Garner, how much are you prepared to pay?'

She turned triumphantly to her husband and gloated: 'There! You see, you fool. I told you she was merely after his money.'

He said nothing, and she turned back to me again. 'Name your own price, Miss Barry.'

'Very well, I will. I'd want at least twenty-five thousand dollars!'

She almost fell over backwards, and stammered: 'T-t-twenty-five?'

'Not one penny less.'

'But — but it's preposterous!'

'Not at all. Your son's a good catch — a fine fish to land, Mrs. Garner. I don't expect I'll ever get hold of another man with half his money, will I? No, twenty-five grand is the price I'm asking to give him up and tell him nothing about our little talk.'

She motioned her husband aside and spoke confidentially to him in one corner. He seemed to be expostulating, but she carried the day, as doubtless she always did. He took out his cheque book and started drawing up a cheque. She blotted it and came over to me with it.

'Here's my husband's cheque for twenty-five thousand dollars, Miss Barry. In return I must ask you never to see my son again, and to leave this house before he returns. You agree?'

I took the cheque and folded it carefully and placed it in my dress top. 'Thank you, Mrs. Garner. I have no doubt if I'd told Reggie of your low tricks, he'd have found it hard to believe me. With this cheque as evidence, he'll know what kind of mother he has. I'm afraid you're making the mistake of thinking that a woman in your position can tread on a girl like me. You're wrong about that, but I can't convince you you are. However, you're not going to stop me marrying Reggie. That's final.'

Reggie's father grinned. 'Told you so, my dear. She's a spirited little devil. Might as well give in and let the thing go through with our blessing. I don't think Reggie'll find anyone else now, at his age, and I doubt if he'll find anyone as suitable as Lucille, in spite of her background.'

'You mean you doubt if he'll find anyone as *degrading* as Lucille!'

'Really, my dear, that's going a bit too far, you know . . . '

'You're quite right, Mr. Garner. It's going too far. You can tell dear Reggie what happened, and why I'm gone when he comes back,' I said. Raging with temper, I turned on my heel and walked out of the room.

* * *

Long before Reggie got back home, I had packed and was ready to leave. I saw his mother watching me going from the library window, and I pretended not to notice her. I walked out of the gates and down the road towards the station.

I didn't feel anything but anger at the moment. Anger against Reggie even, for letting me in for this. But perhaps he hadn't known that other, harsher side of his mother. Still, I was mad at him — now; but something told me that shortly I was going to miss him and feel very lonely without him. I half-decided to stay and explain things to him; I was sure his mother would give him an entirely wrong version of the affair — and there was the cheque in my pocket! Still, I could always address that to him from New York, and leave him to figure out for himself why they'd given it me. Or should I stay? Then that stubborn streak in me came up again, and I walked on determinedly.

I'd covered half the distance to the nearby town when I heard the patter of feet and a panting breath behind me. I turned round hoping it might be Reggie — but it was only his father, red and breathless, waving at me. I stopped and waited for him to come to a gasping halt.

'Silly of you to run away, my dear,' he told me. 'Why not wait and see the boy?'

'No, Mr. Garner. I've decided.'

'Well, then, let me walk you to the station. I dodged out the back way — my wife'd have a fit if she knew I'd gone, but I couldn't see you go like that.'

I smiled at him. 'Thank you, Mr. Garner. It's very kind of you.'

'I don't know what kind of story my wife'll give Reggie,' he said reflectively as we walked along. 'But it'll be something to discredit you. However, you can be certain of one thing: I'm on your side, and as soon as I can manage it I'll take Reggie aside and explain the true story to him. Trust me, Lucille.'

'Do you think it will make any difference?'

'Sure. Reggie isn't tied to his mother's apron strings by any means. She thinks he is, but I know him better than she does. He humours her a lot, and she's gotten into the way of thinking that he depends on her.'

He talked cheerfully on the way to the station, and in no time we were both on the platform waiting for the New York train, which was due almost immediately. Before I stepped aboard he clasped my hand and gave it a warm shake, then leaned over and kissed me in a fatherly way on the cheek. 'I like you, Lucille — and don't forget, Reggie *will* be back. I'll see to that.' He looked a forlorn little figure as the train puffed away, plump and sad, standing on the platform, waving.

At length he was out of sight, and I leaned back in my seat and gave my mind full play. It wasn't a nice journey; I was beginning to realise how much I loved Reggie now there was a danger of losing him. I wished I'd been less headstrong and waited to explain. I wished . . . oh, I wished a million things, but it was too late now for any of my wishes to be granted. I'd taken my course and it was up to me to steer along it. If Reggie really loved me, he'd come back to me in spite of what his mother told him.

I didn't get any sleep on that run back

196

to New York. When I got off at Grand Central Terminal, I was heavy-eyed and feeling weary and tired. My return was so different from the way I'd set off. All the happiness was gone from my life right now. There was only one thought to stimulate me: at least I was back where I really belonged, and I could see Maddie and tell her all my troubles, and she'd comfort me as only she had the power to.

Maddie! One friend who'd stuck by me through thick and thin, and who always would. Who'd been unofficial executioner to the woman who'd beaten me up; who'd risked setting the cops onto Riccy to get him away from me.

I took a cab back to the Bexton. The theatre was deserted, for I'd arrived early in the morning. The door of our suite, which stood right next to the stage door, was closed . . . and there was something funny about it. I knew what it was almost at once.

The milk.

Three days' supply of milk stood on the step; three morning newspapers were jutting from the letterbox.

That was queer; I couldn't understand Maddie not taking in the milk and papers. She was always the first to grab the daily news and read it from end to end. She had a keen interest in life, and what was happening all over the world, even if she didn't understand a lot of the words.

I put my key into the lock and opened the door. Inside, the stairs were dark, lower curtains closed. It looked as if Maddie had not been around for some time. I walked up the stairs after opening the curtains and shedding light on the hallway. The door of the suite itself was slightly ajar, and I called out: 'Maddie — hello, Maddie?'

There was utter silence; I pushed the door right open and went in.

A tray was on the table, beside an opened paper; the coffee in the cups was half-congealed. The clock on the window ledge had stopped at three, but whether a.m. or p.m., I couldn't tell. The calendar beside it, however, stood open at a date *three days* earlier!

My mind was instantly beset by fears

for Maddie. Where was she? Where had she gone? Had she decided, since I was away and likely to be away for some time, to go and stay with one of her boyfriends for the time being? It was possible, but hardly likely, for Maddie had never stayed out all night. Sometimes she'd arrived home from a party or date as late as four a.m., but never later than that.

I went through into the bedroom. The bed was made; had not been slept in. Her pyjamas were lying folded up on the pillow. Her negligee was lying neatly across the back of a chair.

I glanced through her wardrobe and noticed that the dress and coat she wore when going to the show were missing, but no more of her stuff. That was funny; had she been going to spend a few days with one of her sugar daddies, she'd surely have taken her best things.

Worried almost out of my mind, I walked downstairs. My main idea was to go and see Jake the doorman and see if he could give any lead on where she was. Passing the door, I slipped out the three papers, found the latest, and glanced

casually at the headlines. They leapt out
and almost made me faint with shock:

*'FAMOUS BURLESQUITE
MADDIE MARITZA FISHED OUT
OF HUDSON RIVER —
MURDERED!'*

17

Shadows on the Sidewalk

Maddie murdered!

Horrified, I read on, standing where I was, holding the paper screwed up, showing the half-column devoted to the story. It said very little; just gave a brief résumé of her past and present career and the shows and theatres she'd worked in. Then it went on to say that river police had fished her body from the Hudson the previous night. Her heart had been pierced, it said, by a long knife that had been driven into her back. No clues offered themselves, and it was thought that one of her 'friends' might have committed the crime, of which she had several. Enquiries were progressing.

Numbed, unable to think straight, I walked out, still holding the paper. I walked down the street until I reached the main stem, then I boarded a trolley for

Hell's Kitchen, in which our disreputable neighbourhood doorkeeper, Jake, hung out. I found him at home in a stuffy tenement room, sweating in the heat and reading the account of Maddie's death. He stood up as I came in and slipped on his shoes to hide the holes in his socks, put on his jacket over his ragged shirt, and said: 'Take a seat, Miss Barry.'

'I — I won't stay, Jake. I just wanted to ask you a question or two.'

'Certainly, Miss Barry. You've seen this ... ?' he said, indicating the newspaper.

'Yes, Jake. That's what I came about.'

'I'm sorry, miss. She was a grand lady, was Miss Maritza. Too bad she had to go that way.'

'How did it happen? I mean, when? Have you any idea who might've done it?'

'Not unless it's like the paper says, miss. One of them fellers she was fond of rooking.'

'But — surely you knew she was missing? It seems she hasn't been home for days, so she must've missed the show.'

'She did, miss. The last time I seen her

was when that note from Tim Foley came for her, three nights ago. It was delivered by a street kid who said he'd been given it by some feller. It said Tim Foley wanted to see her urgent, and could she come right after the show to his place. She told me what was in it, and said perhaps Foley'd got in trouble and needed her to help him see the way out. She went right after the show.

'Then the following night she never turned up for the overture, and we sent up to the suite for her. The place was locked up; we couldn't get in. Harry, one of the stagehands, climbed up the fire escape and managed to get in by the window. He came back and said she wasn't there. We got in touch with Tim Foley, and he said he never sent any note, and he'd never seen Maddie. It was all a ruse to get her out that late . . . and now they've found her in the river, stabbed to death.'

'I see. When she was definitely found to be missing, didn't you report to the police?'

He shook his head. 'No, miss. You know

yourself what Maddie was, and we figured she was on the loose somewhere. We decided to give her a few days to turn up, and meanwhile we managed to put the show on without her.'

I stood up. 'Thank you, Jake. I see how it all happened now.'

'You don't think it might've been Tim Foley who done it?'

'How could it have been? What motive could he have had?'

'They did say he was very fond of the lady, Miss Barry. He was real cut up when she left.'

'No, I don't for one minute think it was Timmy. He'd never do a thing like that, Jake. I must be going now — I'll see you tonight at the theatre.'

I went right to the police depot, found out where Maddie had been taken, and got permission to see her.

'Here she is,' said the morgue attendant, whipping back a cloth from a sheeted figure. I stood gazing down on her. Her face was calm and serene — it was hard to believe she'd died from violence, perhaps in agony. She was so utterly still and lifeless that when I saw the reality of her death, and knew that big heart would never beat again, my throat swelled up, and hot tears trickled from my eyes and down my cheeks and fell on her still face.

'That's one that won't ever see the pearly gates if what they say's right,' said the attendant with a grin.

I was enraged by his callousness and whirled on him. 'That's where you're wrong. Maddie's bound to go to heaven — whatever she did, she was wonderful under the surface.'

He sniffed. 'Okay lady, don't get het up. I take it back.'

Sick and hopeless, I trailed out of the morgue. How I needed Reggie now, more than ever — to help me over this blow; to soften the harsh impact of Maddie's death. But I was right where I had started from, alone and friendless in New York, drifting aimlessly around the town trying to forget.

I found the nearest restaurant and went in and ordered food. When it came, I sat without touching it, until it went cold and congealed on the plate. I drank strong black coffee, went out into the streets again, and just walked.

How long and how far I walked, I can't remember. I recollect getting as far as downtown Manhattan, and then cutting through again into Chinatown, then along the Bowery, and finally going across the river to Brooklyn. When I decided it was time to get home again, it was dark and late. At last I became aware of the numb ache in my feet and the muscle pains along my calves and legs. I started slowly to retrace my way, took the ferry, and leaned over the rails, watching the water, black and oily and illimitable, flowing turgidly underneath the ship.

I thought of Maddie in the cold lung-bursting embrace, and was thankful she had been dead before she had been thrown in. I wondered who'd done it, and why. I started walking again over the other side, back through Chinatown where the glimmering widely spaced lamps shed long and gruesome shadows on the sidewalk; where women seldom walked alone. But I was past caring about that.

Furtive figures slunk in the shadows as I passed; once, I thought I was being followed, but turning I saw nothing. From a building I passed came the shrill sound of laughter and the sobbing cries of a woman in agony. I wondered if anything like that had happened to Maddie, and shuddered.

I moved out along the Bowery, which was sinister in a different sort of way. It was a place where one was apt to encounter thugs and criminals of the worst types; where the cops never walked except in twos, and never even then if they could help it. Where the starving tramps and decrepit beggars haunted the soup kitchens and mission halls, eking out a paltry, miserable existence, which, too, might end in the river.

The river! Would that be my end, as Maddie had warned me years ago? Would I, frustrated in the one decent love I'd had, turn to lust and wantonness and wild parties, and a gay life if a short one, to ease my aching heart? Subject my physical side to ravages that would ruin me, to eliminate from my mentality the stain it had borne?

I had reached the end of the alley that led to the door of my suite. I paused a while there, afraid of going in and encountering the awful loneliness; the ghost of Maddie hovering above it in every possession of hers I would lay eyes on.

Then I started down the alley; for the only place I could go would have been the theatre and the show, and I couldn't even think of that. With slow, flagging steps, I walked on — and now behind me came other steps, as slow as my own, soft and sinister. I spun around, drawing in a sharp breath. There was a figure behind me — dark, tall figure; the figure of a man in a shapeless brim-down trilby and long black overcoat, collar upturned.

I hastened my steps and paused at the stage door, wondering if I should step inside and lose myself in the warm security of the theatre. Then I knew I couldn't have faced the sympathy I'd have gotten. I walked on quickly, then fitted my key to the door . . .

The man was right behind me. I heard

his breathing by my ear, then felt his hand reach suddenly around my throat and prevent me from calling out. He held me that way while he hissed: 'Okay, take it easy. Just step inside without any fuss, and you won't get hurt — yet!'

I was forced inside, his hand still biting into my windpipe; I thought of kicking backwards, hacking his shins, but discarded the notion at once. That grip on my throat could tighten and strangle the life out of me. And anyhow, I felt strangely detached from the idea of death — impersonal, as if it wasn't really me who was in the grip of God knew what; as if it were someone else, and I was standing by, watching, seeing what decisions the victim would reach.

The decision I did reach was to try nothing. He pushed the door shut behind him and growled: 'Start walking up the stairs. Any funny tricks and I'll fix you good.'

He walked up after me, still holding my throat. It was an awkward way to move, but he took no chances. He kicked open the door of the suite and we went in. He seemed to know his way around. His first move was to click the light switch on; his second to release me, and give me a shove that sent me sprawling helplessly to the floor. Then he kicked me away from him, and I looked up.

'Good God! Riccy!'

'Yes, sure, it's Riccy, you two-faced cheating floozie,' he snarled. His face had altered, gone thin and haggard. A stubbly beard covered his chin, and he had even grown a large moustache. But there wasn't any mistaking his eyes . . . and there wasn't any mistaking his intentions to use the knife he now held in his hand.

I stammered: 'Riccy . . . what do you want?'

He laughed and sat down on the divan. 'Want? That's a good one. There was a time when I wanted you, baby. That's over now. All I want now is to see you where I put your blasted friend.'

'You killed Maddie?'

'Sure I killed her. I fixed it all up. I said I would, didn't I?'

I recoiled from him in horror, crawled to my knees, got to my feet, and backed away. He rapped: 'If you try anything at all I'll let you feel this knife — and I'll take my time about it. What I need now is something to eat and drink. That'll be your last good deed, baby. Fix me something up, huh?' He motioned me towards the kitchen, then followed me in to see that I didn't try to make a break.

I started slicing bread with him watching keenly. I put the coffee percolator on and fished some canned meat out of the ice-box. He went on talking: 'Maybe you thought you'd thrown me for good when you didn't turn up that day outside the Egremont. Maybe you thought the feds would grab me off pretty quick, and you'd be relieved of the worry as well. Or maybe you just didn't worry about it at all. But I was safe all right — I had a fair hideout ready fixed. Trouble is, I began to run out of dough — and then, as an added incentive, I lamped the paper that said you was going to marry some rich guy. So I came back — for three reasons: one, to pick up the money you've made from the Bexton while Poppa's been away; two, to kill that four-flushing jerk Maddie off; and three, to wipe you out along with her. Like it? Quite a programme, ain't it?'

'But can you get away with it, Riccy?'

'Maybe not — but before they take me, you'll get yours, and that'll console me for what's coming. When they strap me in the chair I'll be able to say I didn't leave behind any dame who'd chiseled and cheated me, won't I?'

'Yes, Riccy,' I said calmly. 'I still wouldn't try it, though. Why not take all the money I can dig up here, and get out to your hideout again?'

'So you could sic the cops on me? Nuts.'

We walked back into the sitting room. He took sandwiches and coffee with one hand and held the knife close to me with the other. He made me stay right by him, back to him. I didn't have a chance to put up a fight of any kind. At last he said: 'Turn around.'

I did so, slowly. He had the knife held in front of me now, and was on his feet. His eyes were burning with the killing lust. He snapped: 'Sorry you ditched me now?'

I shook my head. Somehow the prospect of death didn't send me panicky; not even such a death as he might think up. I knew it would be horrible; maybe when the knife bit in I'd scream and cry, and writhe in agony. But until it did, I was still calm and passive, the whole thing unreal to me.

He got hold of my throat and whirled me around, then pressed me down on the divan. I lay staring up into his eyes. He muttered: 'You're a cute little tyke for all that — if I give you a break, will you promise to come with me and play it square in future?'

I shook my head. His face darkened. 'All right — have it your way. Here it comes . . . '

His hand went back with the knife; and simultaneously the door opened and Reggie entered . . .

18

Dreams in the Night

He stood just inside the door, trying to take in the scene. And like a fool I screamed: '*Reggie*!'

Riccy stopped and whirled around. At the same instant Reggie came at him, having sized up the general situation. They met in the centre of the floor, Reggie unarmed, Riccy with that horrible long knife, probably the one that had killed poor Maddie. And the knife came downwards, striking into Reggie's right shoulder, deflected from his heart line only by a quick twist on his part. His hand came up and caught Riccy's wrist. Riccy's other hand wrapped around his throat. Silently, without even grunting, they fought on, with murder in their minds . . .

I sat petrified where I was; my limbs were incapable of movement. It was only when I saw Reggie trip and fall floorwards with Riccy on top of him that I realised under what a disadvantage he was fighting. His right arm was almost useless; seemingly the knife had severed the controlling muscle there in his shoulder, and his efforts to avert Riccy's knife from his body were growing every minute feebler. Blood was welling out from his gashed shoulder onto the floor, and both men were rolling around in it, their suits a wet, reddened mess.

I caught sight of Reggie's eyes over Riccy's shoulder; they held a hopeless look, as if he knew that the struggle couldn't last much longer. He panted: 'Get out of here, Lucille — quick! I — can't hold him — any longer.'

My head whirling, I rushed into the kitchen and glanced around for a weapon. The bread knife was lying where I had left it after cutting Riccy's sandwiches. It was long, and had a serrated edge.

I picked it up.

I gained the sitting room in time to see Reggie's hold on his opponent's wrist break — the knife went up — came down . . .

He groaned, just once. Then, like a woman gone berserk — which I suppose I was — I darted forward and threw myself on top of Riccy, who had been scrambling to his knees. The bread knife plunged down, and down again, and once more. I couldn't stop myself; I was in a frenzy . . .

He made several attempts to break loose, thrashing wildly around the blood-stained floor. But madness lent me the strength I needed to hold him down — and I did.

At last, from sheer exhaustion, I collapsed . . . and lay, spent, for heaven knows how long.

When I dragged myself to life once more, I shifted what had once been Riccy, and pulled Reggie from under him. Besides the stab wound in his shoulder, there was a second right on the heart line. I couldn't distinguish it very well, for his clothing was soaked and smeared with his own and Riccy's blood.

But I didn't need to know it had penetrated his heart to know that he was dead!

He had come back to me — in time to

save me from a ghastly fate, but in time to suffer in my place!

Faintness swirled over me again; I felt myself crashing down beside him . . .

I remember very little of the period after that. Only that I came to at last, sometime the following day, and struggled over to the phone, and dialed police headquarters.

The court case was a sensation; both the lawyer for my defence and the prosecuting attorney were masters of their game. My own counsel didn't try to deny the murder altogether; he freely admitted I'd killed Ricardo Corday, and based his plea on self-defence. For days the battle waged backwards and forwards; half the public believed that I should get the chair, while the other half said I should get a medal. The former group said I might have killed in self-defence, although they doubted even that; but that my past spoke for itself, and that indirectly I was responsible for the death of Reggie, and Maddie too, apart from Riccy. And so it went on, with my supporters arguing that I had been fully justified in killing him whether it was self-defence or not.

In his summing up, the judge was plainly on my side. He said gravely: 'You have heard the evidence of the prosecution and the accused. On that evidence you will — without any pressure from any source — decide whether the prisoner is guilty or not guilty. Murder is never justified; but when committed in self-defence, it can no longer be classed as murder.

'You must decide, from the evidence you have heard, if this woman stood in danger herself. You must not allow the fact of her profession to prejudice you, nor the fact that she associated in the past with Ricardo Corday, the murdered man. That is not relevant to the decision you have to make. You are trying the defendant on a straight issue — did she, or did she not, murder Ricardo Corday, willfully and maliciously, or did she merely defend herself from a vicious attack that could have resulted only in her own death?

'We have only the prisoner's word that Ricardo Corday killed her friend, Maddie

Maritza. But in view of the murdered man's reputation, this is exceedingly likely. There is nothing more to be said. Members of the jury, you may retire to consider your verdict — and may God guide you.'

The jury filed out, and the court adjourned. They were out, all told, three hours. I didn't care much one way or the other. I didn't care if I died — I wanted to.

When the court assembled again to hear the verdict, there was a breathless, tense hush over the room. The judge said gravely: 'Members of the jury, have you reached your verdict?'

The foreman stood up. He was a small, stunted man; probably a grocer, butcher, or baker, something like that, in private life. But his new office invested him with a certain dignity. He said: 'We have, your honour.'

'The prisoner will rise and face the court.'

I was helped up by two wards.

'Please inform the court of your verdict.'

The foreman cleared his throat and glanced across at me. Then he said: 'We the jury find the defendant *not guilty*.'

And then I passed clean out again . . .

⋆　⋆　⋆

Well, that's my story — the true inside story. I don't care what you may have read at the time; that's on the level. I've told you everything and held back nothing. The publicity I got was too much for me; I quit burlesque and I quit the Bexton, and the old place began to sink. I bought a café and stayed clear of the public eye myself, letting the staff run it. They robbed me, and I lost all I had as years went by. Long after the trial I was still haunted by reporters, editors and publishers, all offering money for my story. But I didn't feel up to it. There was one guy who just stuck and stuck, and who wouldn't take no for answer — he never got the story, but he did, eventually, get *me*. I married him.

That guy was Larsen, the reporter I once had thrown out of my suite!

I've had a lot of happiness with him, and I don't grumble. But for Reggie, I'd have died years ago . . .

But you folks can judge me for yourselves. I've held nothing back, nothing at all. Maybe you think I've been a heel at times, and maybe you think I'm bad all through and should have got the chair anyway. That's up to you . . .

But don't think I haven't been punished.

I may have married Larsen, but I always think of Reggie! I always will! And sometimes I have dreams in the night — dreams where Reggie is there, and we're happy. But they always turn into nightmares, for Riccy always comes too — and at that point Larsen wakes me up, to tell me I've been shrieking!

I never tell him why . . .

We do hope that you have enjoyed reading this large print book.

Did you know that all of our titles are available for purchase?

We publish a wide range of high quality large print books including:
Romances, Mysteries, Classics
General Fiction
Non Fiction and Westerns

Special interest titles available in large print are:
The Little Oxford Dictionary
Music Book, Song Book
Hymn Book, Service Book

Also available from us courtesy of Oxford University Press:
Young Readers' Dictionary
(large print edition)
Young Readers' Thesaurus
(large print edition)

For further information or a free brochure, please contact us at:
Ulverscroft Large Print Books Ltd.,
The Green, Bradgate Road, Anstey,
Leicester, LE7 7FU, England.
Tel: (00 44) **0116 236 4325**
Fax: (00 44) **0116 234 0205**

Mrs. Rampage lives alone, in a large house cluttered with her precious objets d'art. Her daughter is half a world away, and her niece has no time for the old lady. So Mrs. Rampage is persuaded — much against her will — to take a companion into her home: Mrs. Roach, a poor but respectable widow. As resentment mounts between the pair, a violent confrontation is inevitable when the suppressed tension finally boils over . . .

SHERLOCK HOLMES AND MR. MAC

Gary Lovisi

'Mr. Mac', as Sherlock Holmes calls him, is the talented young Inspector Alec MacDonald. Though he's out to make his mark at Scotland Yard, some baffling new cases have him seeking assistance from the great detective; and the two, along with the stalwart Doctor Watson, join forces. In *The Affair of Lady Westcott's Lost Ruby*, the seemingly mundane disappearance of an elderly lady's pet leads to unexpectedly sinister consequences, while in *The Unseen Assassin*, a mysterious marksman embarks upon a serial killing spree across London.

BACKGROUND FOR MURDER

Shelley Smith

In a psychiatric hospital, the head doctor lies dead — his skull smashed in with a brass poker. Private investigator Jacob Chaos is called in by Scotland Yard to investigate. But there are many people who might have wished harm upon Dr. Royd: the patients who resented his cruel treatment methods; the doctors who harboured jealousy of his position; even his own wife. With Dr. Helen Crawford as the Watson to his Holmes, Chaos must untangle the threads of the mystery . . .

THE RELUCTANT WITNESS

Mary Wickizer Burgess

Attorney Gail Brevard is faced with a big problem when her key witness, Clinton Bolt, goes on the lam to Mexico. An arson death and an unexpected kidnapping are just a few of the issues she and her colleagues must deal with while preparing for a trial with millions of dollars at stake. A whirlwind trip across the border gives Gail the upper hand — but not for long, as the criminals are still at large. Where will the unknown assailant strike next — and who will be the next victim?